Our Leaders Are Stupid!

The Political Speeches
Donald J. Trump
Wishes He'd Made

Franco "Pancho" Bahamonde

Illustrated by John Clifton

Publication date: November 2015.

CONTENTS

Preface

These are the political speeches Donald Trump would give if Donald Trump used a TelePrompTer. But because he does not use a TelePrompTer, there is a sense of disconnect between what's in his mind and what comes out of his mouth.

These speeches connect his mind and his mouth as never before, relieving the American public from having to avail itself of telepathy to understand fully what Donald Trump means when he opens his mouth and speaks and speaks and speaks in a manner reminiscent of Fidel Castro who spoke and spoke and spoke for hours without uttering a single complete sentence. Or complete thought.

Donald Trump's sentences are now herein rendered complete. And so are his thoughts, if not in streams of consciousness then in streams of consciouslessness.

After all, when Donald Trump said that Mexicans going to the U.S. are taking drugs, and taking crime, and they're rapists—he forgot to mention that they're also sending books.

Books like this one! Books that mock the monolingual mogul! You're welcome, America!

Franco "Pancho" Bahamonde
Mérida, Yucatán

1

1. Why Hillary Cannot Be President!

Our leaders are stupid!

That's why the United States, once the greatest nation on earth, is such a mess. And *that* mess is the legacy of the Clinton and Bush presidencies.

And now Hillary wants to be president?

Can you imagine? Can you imagine?

Can you imagine the *nightmare* that that would be?

Hillary was a terrible senator for New York State. She promised 500,000 jobs in New York State—and she didn't deliver on that.

She lied. She lied about the jobs she would bring to New York State. That's because she was an incompetent senator.

She did nothing for New York State! She only used New York as a platform for her ambitions, just like every other carpetbagger in history has done!

And, by the way, Hillary did a terrible job as secretary of state as well. One ambassador was killed by terrorists and we have now more enemies than we did before she went to the State Department.

Can you imagine?

One of our embassies was destroyed by terrorists under her watch—after she refused to provide security to our ambassador who was desperate, I mean desperate, for more protection.

It's a tragedy, a tragedy.

This is what we get when we have stupid, stupid people in office.

Let me be clear: Hillary has terrible, terrible judgment.

Using a private server for her emails is just one more example of her poor judgment, her sense of self-importance, her belief that the rules don't apply to her, and her phenomenal arrogance.

Now, I'm not modest, I know.

But I'm not modest because I have achievements of my own!

Where are *her* achievements?

It isn't bringing jobs to New York State. It isn't making America's foreign policy stronger.

What has she done?

Apart from stealing whatever she could steal wherever she could steal it?

From the Rose law firm to the Clinton Foundation's shakedown of the rich and stupid, that's where her money has come from. Do you want a president in the White House whose foundation received millions and millions of dollars from despots around the world—like the corrupt despot running Saudi Arabia, King Abdul bin Corrupt al-Tyrant?

Now, I'm rich. I'm really rich. I'm really, really rich.

But I made my billions through my world-class skills as a world-class businessman, a businessman visionary, if you want to know the truth.

Believe me, Hillary is not brilliant.

And she's not a good negotiator. She couldn't negotiate anything to bring jobs in New York State. She couldn't negotiate with our friends—forget about negotiating with our enemies.

Proof? I have two words: Iran Deal!

What a disaster!

And because of her lack of judgment, Hillary has some very, very big problems.

And the biggest problem is her terrible, terrible judgment.

Look at decisions in every aspect of her life. She stuck by Bill after Bill was screwing an intern in the Oval Office. She did nothing, nothing, nothing about Benghazi and our ambassador was murdered—along with other patriots.

And that email server!

What was she thinking? That *her* security is tighter than the State Department's?

Give *me* a break! Give *America* a break!

It's up to Congress to decide if she committed a crime—which by the way, Congress is investigating!

I don't think she can be president. I think she should get the same—if not *more*—punishment than General David Petraeus, but that's just my opinion.

What is not *my* opinion, because it is fact, is that Hillary has terrible, terrible judgment!

Fact: Who does she surround herself with?

Huma Abedin, the Muslim confidant to Hillary.

Huma, Okay?

Who is Huma?

Here's a story about Huma. She is one of the stupid, stupid, stupid people involved in this outrageous, outrageous server "I-couldn't-deal-with-two-email-accounts-so-I-just-had-my-own-server" scandal.

Huma told Hillary that having her own private server was a brilliant idea. And that's why Hillary's campaign is dying the death of a thousand disclosures, the death of a thousand emails!

So Huma is in the Clinton campaign's inner circle. In fact, Hillary has said she considers Huma to be like a daughter.

If that's the case . . .

Well, *who* is Huma married to?

One of the great sleazebags of our time: Anthony Weiner!

Did you know that?

She's married to Anthony Weiner!

You know, the Bing! Bing! Bing! Bong! Bong! Bong!

And there goes a selfie of his erection off into cyberspace—SEXTING!

And it's out there in cyberspace forever!

Did you know you can Google Anthony Weiner's penis and see it? This is the *disgusting* human trash that Hillary wants to take with her to the White House! Huma and Anthony!

Think about it!

Here's a guy who has to resign from Congress because he's sending pictures of his privates to all his "I Love You Very Much" girlfriends online!

Think of it!

Huma is getting all this classified information, and she's married to Anthony Weiner, who's a Perv!

No, he is!

The man's a Perv!

What does this say about Huma's judgment? She didn't divorce this man after his perversions were revealed and he was forced to resign from Congress.

Makes sense in a way: Hillary stood by Bill after his cigar-sex interlude with Monica Lewinsky was revealed!

Huma and Hillary.

Hillary and Huma.

Two sick fucks.

Can you imagine if Hillary is elected to office?

Think of it!

If she considers Huma to be like her daughter, then that means that Hillary and Bill must consider Anthony Weiner to be like a son-in-law!

Can you imagine Bill and Anthony in the White House!

I can. I can.

I can tell you *exactly* the scandal that will hit American in 2017 or 2018 if Hillary is president.

End of year, Christmas party for the staff—even if Huma is a Muslim and Anthony is a Jew—both will attend because they are like a daughter and son-in-law to Hillary, the woman with impaired judgment.

And they're at the White House for the staff Christmas party— and Hillary is reminiscing about all the places Monica Lewinsky gave Bill a blow job.

And while all are having a grand ol' Christmas party time of it, Anthony Weiner slips away and wanders over to the Oval Office.

Now, does anyone here believe that that Perv won't be able to resist temptation?

You know what I'm talking about. You know what that Perv will do if he is ever in the Oval Office by himself for a moment.

Out comes the cell phone and down goes the zipper!

Selfies of Anthony Weiner's wiener live from the Oval Office are going to be sexted all over the place!

Bing! Bing! Bing! Bong! Bong! Bong! "I Love You Very Much from the Oval Office!"

That's what America is setting itself up for if Hillary is elected! Can you imagine! Can you imagine! Can you imagine!

So then, Bill and his cigars and Anthony and his selfies are wandering around the White House.

Is this what America wants?

Bill, the First Perv, who has no respect for women—just ask Monica. Anthony, the Son-in-Law Perv, who has no respect for his wife—did you know he did it again after he was caught and he promised not to do it again?

You didn't know?

Anthony Weiner was caught sending selfies of his wiener while in Congress. He resigns, he cries, he promises never to do it again. Huma believes the Perv's lies. Then he thinks he has rehabilitated himself enough—to run for Mayor of New York.

It's true!

That sick Perv wanted to follow Michael Bloomberg! One Perv Jew to follow one fantastic Jewish businessman who did a great deal to turn New York around!

And guess what?

In July 2013, Anthony "The Perv" Weiner was caught doing it again! His alias was "Carlos Danger" and selfies of his wiener were all over the place!

Again!

Google his name and you find more pics of his penis!

Disgusting!

Huma, betrayed, humiliated, and shamed, still stays married to the Perv.

Again, that tells me she's nuts. That woman is nuts, just another crazy Muslim who submits to the will of her Perv husband!

No self-respect! No self-respect!

And Huma, the crazy Muslim married to the Jewish Perv, is giving Hillary *advice* because Hillary considers this crazy Muslim who's married to a Jewish Perv to be like a daughter!

Give *me* a break! Give *America* a break!

America deserves better than this. America will never be great again if we have this kind of filth in the White House.

Bill and Anthony.

Anthony and Bill.

Two sick Pervs.

And while Bill is out there with his cigars and Anthony is busy taking selfies of his privates, the country is going down the toilet.

I'll bet you anything Huma told Hillary it was a great idea to have a private server. I'll bet you anything Huma told Hillary that Hillary looks great in blue pantsuits.

Hillary has millions and millions and millions of dollars. She can *afford* to have a personal shopper and a fashion consultant. She can afford to look good.

That's why King Abdul bin Corrupt al-Tyrant gave the Clinton Foundation millions and millions of dollars! So, in the eventuality that she's president, King Abdul bin Corrupt al-Tyrant will have an American president indebted to him!

King Abdul bin Corrupt al-Tyrant also gave Hillary millions of dollars so she could have an age-appropriate wardrobe!

It's true!

Look, she doesn't have to hire that old guy from *Project Runway*—that gay Tim Gunn guy. Which, by the way, Tim Gunn could be doing Heidi Klum a favor by helping her, you know, camouflage.

Heidi was once a Ten—I'm sure we can all agree on that.

But now? She's an Eight—and I'm sure we can all agree on that also.

8

But that gay Tim Gunn guy isn't doing her any favors by not helping her camouflage her sagging body. She could be back to being a Nine if she had better fashion advice.

That can also be said of Hillary. Of course Hillary has never been more than a Four. She's a Two now, but with help, she could pass for a Three.

I'll bet, as I've said, that Huma is the one who told Hillary that she looks great in blue pantsuits.

Well, Hillary, if you're listening, I'm going to tell it to you straight: *You don't.*

You have Hippo Hips that need to be camouflaged.

If you want, as a gesture of friendship—she and Bill attended my wedding in Florida, by the way, full disclosure there—I'll have my daughter Ivanka. My daughter is beautiful and a fashion icon, if you want to know the truth. I'll ask her to send you a style consultant.

But anyway!

When Hillary's dressed in blue, she looks like a giant, fat blue robin.

Hillary Hippo Hips need to be camouflaged, the same way Huma the crazy Muslim needs to come to her senses and divorce that Jew Perv.

Now, I'm not perfect.

Who is?

I may not be perfect, but I don't have crazy people with insane judgment working for me!

That's who Hillary has working for her: Crazy people with insane judgment!

I don't have self-loathing women who have no self-respect working for me!

That's what they are! That's what Hillary and Huma are!

Hillary has no self-respect to stay married to a man who violated Monica the way Bill violated Monica! And Huma has no self-respect to stay married to a Perv who lied to her twice.

You know, it's possible for women to be misogynistic.

9

It's true.

Women can hate women. I believe that Hillary and Huma are misogynists.

In my life, in my business, and in my career I have hired more women executives than men executives.

Women executives, they love me! All my executives, they love me!

And in all the decades I have been in business — making billions of dollars and creating thousands of jobs — not once has there been sex scandal! Never, ever has there been an accusation of anything untoward in how I, or how my company, have treated women.

Why?

Because I love women — I've been married to three wonderful women — and I am blessed to have two beautiful daughters — Ivanka and Tiffany.

And I am a gentleman to all women, even fat pigs like Rosie O'Donnell.

Why?

Because I have always treated women with respect, and I have always promoted women to positions of authority and responsibility.

I love women and — more importantly — I cherish and respect women.

And because I respect women I can tell you right here and right now that Hillary in the office would be a disaster!

Everything about her is phony. When she finally came clean and admitted that it was a "mistake" — a "mistake" — to have her own server, she did so — when?

Six hundred sixty-six days after the scandal broke!

And let me tell you something. She wasn't sincere when she said, "I'm sorry."

It was a *political* calculation: Hillary was only willing to admit that having a private server was a mistake *after* her poll numbers *tanked!*

Believe me! Believe me when I say that had her polls numbers *not* been in free fall, she wouldn't have admitted that that mistake was a mistake.

Hillary's not sorry! She's just sorry that her numbers are tanking!

Now that her numbers show the public realizes she's a loser, she's attacking me.

She's become mean and nasty.

And, quite frankly, she's become a bitch.

And she's become meaner and bitchier as her numbers have tanked.

When a dismal socialist like Bernie Sanders is giving her a run for her money, well, then you know she's in trouble.

And Hillary is in trouble—just her record as secretary of state is enough to make one vomit.

Under her watch, ISIS has taken over Iraq and Syria. Under her watch, we have betrayed those Iraqi and Afghan interpreters and translators who believed in us. Under her watch, the Russians and Chinese have launched wave after wave of cyber attacks against our country. Under her watch, we have lost everyone's respect!

She's a loser!

She certainly got her cellulite-laden ass kicked by Barack Obama back in 2008! And because she's a loser, America has become a loser nation.

Well, I'm a winner!

I'm a ten-billion dollar winner!

And I'm going to make America a winner again!

That's something Hillary will never be able to do.

I mean, look at her! She's still explaining shit about that server and her emails. It goes on and on and one—except, of course, on *Saturday Night Live.*

On that show, you know they all support her so they give her a free ride.

Do we want a president who's going to spend every waking hour talking about an email account? That's what Bill did in his second term—spent the entire time talking about what the meaning of "is" is or was—and where Monica did or did not give him a blow job.

Who wants that?

Who wants to hear Hillary Hippo Hips talk about being sorry about using a private server for the next four years?

Give *me* a break! Give *America* a break!

Quite frankly, had she been "sorry," she would have been sorry on the first day! Not on the 666th day of the scandal!

She's a phony, and for her to expect women to believe her insincere "sincerity" is an act of aggression against women!

Let's add another *H* to her name: Hypocrite!

Hillary Hippo Hips Hypocrite!

Six hundred and sixty-six days into the scandal, that's when she apologized! That's the number of the beast!

And that's also the number for Hillary Hippo Hips Hypocrite, dressed in a blue pantsuit that makes her look like a giant, fat blue robin!

Did you see her on the *Ellen* show? She looked like a giant, fat blue robin—about to lay eggs!

That's her entire campaign: Hillary Hippo Hips Hypocrite, looking like a giant, fat blue robin, laying one egg after another!

America deserves better! America deserves an eagle, not a robin!

We cannot set women back decades by having Hillary Hippo Hips Hypocrite elected to office!

That would put Bill the First Perv and Anthony the Son-in-Law Perv near the Oval Office!

It would be an act of misogyny to vote for Hillary!

We can't! We can't elect Hillary Hippo Hips Hypocrite to anything other than the Worst-Dressed List!

And, more importantly, we can't have a vicious person as president. Despite how I may come across, I'm a nice person.

I am!

I treat everyone well. Very well.

I'm the best boss and the best tipper in the world.

But Hillary?

Don't take it from me. Take it from the Secret Service agents who had to endure her temper.

Ronald Kessler's new book, *First Family Detail*, gives a compelling look at the *real* Hillary Clinton when the news cameras are off.

He writes: "When in public, Hillary smiles and acts graciously. But as soon as the cameras are gone, her angry personality, nastiness, and imperiousness become evident."

We can't have someone like that in the Oval Office.

And we certainly can't have someone who has the poor judgment to dress up like a giant, fat blue robin!

No more Clintons! No more bad judgment!

Make America Great Again!

Vote Trump.

2. We Need a Wall on the Border!

Our leaders are stupid!

Bush I! Clinton! Bush II! Obama!

They have done nothing, absolutely nothing to control our border with Mexico.

Let me tell you something: We need a wall.

We need a wall *yesterday!*

And it will be good for us and it will be good for Mexico. That's why Mexico will be happy to pay for it and we will be happy to patrol it.

Believe me, I know how to build things!

It will be a beautiful wall. It will be so beautiful that it will become a tourist attraction.

People from around the world will travel to the U.S. just to see the wall, the way people today go to China to see the Great Wall of China.

Well, it's time we had a Great Wall of America!

Let me tell you something. I will build the best wall, the biggest, the strongest, not penetrable, they won't be crawling over it, like giving it a little jump and they're over the wall.

It costs us trillions right now, not having a wall.

Let me tell you something else: Mexico will be happy with that wall!

Do you think Mexico is happy with what's going on?

I'll bet you think that most of the people crossing the border—*the illegals*—are Mexicans.

Guess what?

They're not!

They're not Mexicans!

Most of the illegals coming over are from elsewhere.

Why?

Because Mexico can't control *its* southern border with Guatemala and Belize!

And *we* can't control our border with Mexico!

It's true!

The same way the U.S. can't control its southern border with Mexico, Mexico can't control its border with Guatemala and Belize!

Tens of thousands of people are crossing Mexico's southern border, traveling through Mexico, and then entering the U.S.

When we have a wall, then everyone will know the wall is there—and that it's pointless to try to break through it.

It's a dead end. They will know they won't be able to get through it.

The wall will be a world-class deterrent!

That's right! The wall will be a deterrent.

When the wall's up, people from the world over won't cross *into* Mexico from Guatemala or Belize when they know it's useless trying to make it north *to* the U.S.-Mexico border.

And I'm not talking of a few thousand people.

Did you know that last year more than 14,000 Cubans *walked* into the U.S. from Mexico? How did that happen? Cuba's an island!

But somehow they got themselves from Cuba to Mexico and then got on buses and ended up at the border.

They *walked* into the U.S.—from *Cuba!*

Out!

Of!

Control!

People are pouring across our borders, which is horrible.

When I'm president, I'm building a wall.

We have to build a wall.

And I'm the man to do it.

Look, I build some of the greatest buildings in the world. Building a wall is easy for me. It will be a *real* wall. Not a wall that people walk over.

Of course, when I say this, all the Latinos in the media—who are media whores and want me to boost the ratings for their terrible, terrible shows—cry that it's ridiculous.

"Oh, you can't build a wall!" they say.

Why not?

China built a wall.

We need a wall!

And do you know what?

Mexico wants a wall!

They may not know it, but when they see the benefits of it, they will love it and they will thank the U.S.

Let me tell you something about being a successful businessman and a visionary, since I'm both.

I didn't make billions and billions of dollars by *not* knowing how business works or by not being a visionary.

There are times when you have to jump steps ahead and see what others can't see.

Look, no one woke up one day and said, "Oh, I'd like to use my telephone to read the *New York Times*."

And if you had had a focus group asking people if they wanted to read the *New York Times* with their telephones, they would have said you were nuts.

Well, guess what?

There was a businessman visionary—like I'm a businessman visionary—who knew that people wanted to read the *New York Times* on their telephones.

And take pictures with their phones, and find out what the weather was going to be like with their phones, and do math on calculators on their phones, and make videos with their phones, and listen to music on their phones, and take credit card payments with their phones—and all other kinds of wonderful things.

Only they didn't know they wanted it!

His name was Steve Jobs.

And do you know what he said about focus groups and asking

people what they want?

He said that for something that's complicated, and I quote my fellow businessman visionary here, "It's really hard to design products by focus groups!"

He went on!

He said, "A lot of times, people don't know what they want until you show it to them."

Listen to that again: *A lot of times, people don't know what they want until you show it to them.*

You didn't know you *wanted* an iPhone *until* Steve Jobs *showed* you an iPhone.

If Apple had relied on focus groups, it wouldn't have invented the iPhone.

Why? Because nobody wanted a telephone they could use to read the *New York Times!*

Mexico doesn't know it wants the wall until we show them the *benefits* of having a wall.

And there are many benefits!

For us, in America, it's a no-brainer: We can secure our borders after decades and decades of failed administrations that have not been able to secure the border with Mexico.

Bush I! Clinton! Bush II! Obama!

Disasters! One and all!

Quite frankly, we have had the worst presidents this century that America has ever had: Bush II and Obama!

That's why America now desperately needs my bravado and business savvy.

But for Mexico—listen, the Mexicans are under an *invasion* by *millions* of people that *enter* Mexico illegally, or under false pretenses, only to make it to the U.S.

And the result is a terrible, terrible humanitarian crisis!

Do I need to remind everyone here of what's going on down at the border *right now?*

The Department of Homeland Security has detained more than

52,000 unaccompanied children at the border. These are kids from families so desperate to get them out of harm's way in Guatemala or El Salvador that they send them to the U.S.

Alone!

Why?

Because in those countries, once a kid becomes a teenager, they have two choices: Join a criminal gang, or be shot dead.

So the parents, fearing for their children, send them to the U.S. knowing that there are sanctuary cities that will take care of them!

Do you know who's behind these sanctuary cities?

Leftist Losers.

Dianne Feinstein, when she was mayor of San Francisco, championed them.

Look, in American history sometimes people have advanced their otherwise pathetic political careers through political assassination.

Sad, but true. Had McKinley not been assassinated, Teddy Roosevelt wouldn't have become president. Had Kennedy not been killed, LBJ wouldn't have become president.

How stupid is Dianne Feinstein?

Let me tell you!

It took *two* assassinations—George Moscone and Harvey Milk— to get her to become *mayor* of San Francisco.

That's pretty stupid if you need a *double assassination* to move your political career along.

And then, as mayor of that loser city, she encourages immigration lawlessness!

Yes, that's right!

She goes along with San Francisco declaring itself a Sanctuary City—telegraphing to everyone in Latin America that they'll be protected in violation of federal immigration laws!

That crazy Jew was acting as if we're talking about *persecuted* Jews fleeing the Nazis!

That, I could understand.

But *economic* refugees from Latin America are *not* fleeing a Holocaust!

This human wave of unaccompanied children is part of the immigration crisis overtaking our country!

Barack Obama called it a humanitarian crisis. Then he went to Camp David to play golf.

What a leader!

No wonder the country is such a mess!

But it doesn't stop there.

What does Congress do? Nothing!

Our leaders are stupid! There's a crisis of unimaginable proportions, and Obama heads off to play golf and Congress goes into recess.

The entire mess is left in the hands of the states—and the courts.

We're seeing the images of hundreds of thousands of Syrians flooding into Europe desperate to escape civil war—and we're horrified.

Meanwhile, Homeland Security is housing tens of thousands of children—*children*—in makeshift detention centers and warehouses for kids, and the media is too busy talking about my hair!

What kind of country have we become when we have thousands of children in internment camps, detention centers, and warehouses for kids?

Where is the media?

That tells you the lack of professional seriousness in the media today!

We have 52,000 children in internment camps along our border with Mexico, and CNN has Breaking News about my hair.

What bullshit!

What is forgotten in this mess is that these children didn't materialize on the border because Scotty beamed them down from the Starship Enterprise!

No!

They had to travel *through* Mexico!

Do you think Mexico is happy about that? Do you think Mexico is happy about hundreds of thousands of people trampling through its country to make it to the border?

Of course they're not happy about it.

And — hey, I love Mexico and I love the Mexican people, which is why I want to help them solve this crisis that's also tearing their country apart.

One of the qualities that has made me very successful as a negotiator, as businessman, and as a philanthropist, is my ability to empathize.

It's true.

A deal cannot be *successful* unless *both* parties are better off.

It has to be a win-win situation because deals that are win-lose fall apart.

Right now, even as I speak, there are thousands of people crossing the border *into* Mexico *from* Guatemala and Belize. Then they make their way to towns large and small. They board buses. They hook up with smugglers driving vans. They hop on trains.

Trains.

I want to talk about the trains.

Once in Mexico, these illegals take the train that takes them from the south of the country to the U.S.–Mexico border.

Do you know what Mexicans call this train?

LAH-BEHS-TI-AH.

La Bestia. The Beast.

We call it the Death Train.

Why?

There are so many illegals riding on the roofs of the train cars that some of them fall off — and they fall to their deaths.

People are run over by the train. Families are separated. Young men are robbed. Young women are raped.

It's horrible, horrible.

So I ask you: What's up with this train?

Call it La Bestia or the Death Train, who's running it?

Are you ready for a surprise?

That train—the one that takes illegals from Mexico's south to *our* border—is an American train!

It's known as the NAFTA Railroad—which, by the way, was a terrible, terrible trade deal—and the owner is Kansas City Southern.

An American train is taking tens of thousands of illegals to our border!

And here is where our terrible trade deals meet terrible immigration policies.

Why does an American company want to own a train that runs through Mexico?

China!

Kansas City Southern wanted to have greater access to Mexico's deepwater port at Lázaro Cárdenas. It wanted an alternative route for the thousands of Chinese companies shipping containers to the U.S.

That's right!

We are buying so many things from China, that the port of Long Beach, California, can't handle any more ships. So now the ships are going to the *Mexican* port of Lázaro Cárdenas and from *there*, they're put on *trains* to the U.S.

Unbelievable! This is unbelievable!

And to make matters worse, these trains are also bringing tens of thousands of illegals to the border!

Now, can it get worse?

Yes, it gets worse!

How?

The disorder, social chaos, and terrible consequences of human trafficking are wreaking havoc in Mexico.

It's so bad that Mexican States are *suing* the train company!

In March 2014, the Attorney General for Veracruz State, Luis Ángel Bravo, filed a criminal complaint with federal prosecutors against the Kansas City Southern de México and Ferrosur!

A *Mexican* Attorney General accused the *American* train

company of criminal behavior against the migrants, including robbery, human trafficking, kidnapping, murder, extortion, and rape.

This is insane!

Our leaders are stupid to let this happen!

American companies are contributing to a humanitarian crisis in Mexico and an immigration crisis on the border!

Can you believe this immigration chaos under Obama?

And the media? Where is the media reporting on all of this chaos?

Where is Jorge Ramos, the self-proclaimed voice of the voiceless? Nowhere! That's where! Nowhere!

There's an organization in Washington called the Washington Office of Latin America, WOLA. This group, WOLA, is a nongovernmental organization.

I have their statement on this situation right here.

It says, in their report, the following: "Migrants in the southern border zone are drawn to 'La Bestia,' the train that heads northward to central Mexico and then on to the U.S. border. For hundreds of miles they ride on the roofs of the train cars trying to avoid fatal falls, hot days, frigid nights, and low-clearance tunnels. Every eight to ten days or so, trains depart from two routes that originate near the southern border."

It goes on to conclude: "The stunning frequency of kidnapping, extortion, human trafficking, rape, and homicide puts Central American migrants' plight in Mexico atop the list of the Western Hemisphere's worst humanitarian emergencies."

A humanitarian emergency in Mexico. An immigration crisis in the U.S.

We have 52,000 unaccompanied children in detention centers. We have millions of illegals entering our country.

And sanctuary cities encourage illegals willing to risk their lives — *and the lives of their children* — to get them to all these scofflaw mayors in these lawbreaking cities.

My administration will arrest the mayors of these sanctuary

cities so they can explain to federal judges on whose authority they are violating the federal immigration laws of this country!

Sanctuary cities in the U.S. are why Mexico itself is confronting an immigration crisis.

And what does the American train company have to say?

I have here the statement from C. Doniele Carlson, their Assistant Vice President for Corporate Communications. It reads: "KCSM complies strictly with the security laws and regulations maintaining close coordination with Mexican and U.S. federal immigration and security authorities. KCSM has regulations for its security crews who must respect the physical integrity of any person who might gain access to one of its trains traveling illegally on the railway. KCSM has made significant investments during past years to increase the security of railway operations in terms of technology, security staff, intelligence, as well as operating systems related to security in stations, shipping points and the main points of our railway network to prevent this kind of illegal activity with success."

Can you believe this? Can you believe any of this?

This all ends when I'm president!

Day 1 in office, this ends!

Day 1 in office, that train stops!

Day 1 in office, the wall begins to rise!

Day 1 in office, sanctuary cities end!

Mexico doesn't want the wall?

The *hell* Mexico doesn't want a wall!

Mexico doesn't know *how much* it wants the wall!

Mexico will be so happy when the wall is up that they will thank us!

Mexico, in fact, will ask us to build a wall on *their* border with Guatemala and Belize!

And, by the way, the same wall that will keep people from entering the U.S. illegally will also keep people we don't want to leave from fleeing the law.

What do I mean?

That American fugitives escape into Mexico to evade American justice.

Did you know there are thousands and thousands of criminals, cop killers, rapists, scam artists, and murderers hiding in Mexico?

For Mexico, it's a nightmare to be a magnet that attracts American fugitives.

Does Mexico want to have thousands of American murderers, pedophiles, rapists, and criminals tramping all over the place?

Of course not!

A wall will prevent American fugitives from fleeing into Mexico.

Does Mexico want a wall?

Mexico doesn't know *how much* it wants a wall—just like you didn't know how much you wanted a smart phone until Steve Jobs, my fellow businessman visionary, showed you the iPhone.

Believe me, when the wall is up, Mexico will wonder how it ever got along without it!

The wall is good for America and it is good for Mexico.

The stupid Latino media that criticize me don't get it.

Jorge Ramos at Univision doesn't get it—he's stupid, stupid, stupid!

You want me to speak Spanish like Low-Energy Loser Jeb speaks Spanish?

Okay, listen up, Jorge and Univision: *¡Jorge Ramos es estúpido!*

Yes, the Latino media are too stupid to connect the dots.

So I'll connect the dots for you!

Jorge Ramos, listen up!

Out-of-Control Borders = An Immigration Crisis in Mexico = La Bestia Death Train = Thousands of Unaccompanied Children Arriving in America = Millions in Social Welfare and Health Care Expenses in Sanctuary Cities = Chaos!

Is that so hard, Jorge?

Out-of-Control Borders = Chaos!

If you don't get it, then schools in Mexico are worse than I thought!

But for everyone who has a brain and can follow logic and has common sense, it's not hard to see that and all these problems—that cost billions and billions of dollars—can be solved by a wall that secures the border!

Walls don't work?

Ask Israel if walls don't work!

A WALL!

America needs it and Mexico will love it!

Make America Great Again!

Vote Trump.

3. Why America Can't Afford More Losers Like Jeb and Carly!

Our leaders are stupid!

How America the Great became America the Mess is the result of our stupid, stupid leaders.

Everyone beats us!

China beats us! Mexico beats us! France beats us!

Believe me, I love China! I love Mexico! I love France!

But we cannot continue to keep losing.

And we're losing because we have losers for leaders.

In this election we are confronting the false choice of picking from a bunch of losers—and a winner.

I'm a winner.

I've made billions and billions of dollars by winning.

The Art of the Deal! The Art of Negotiating! The Art of Winning!

But look who's running against me.

Jeb.

Talk about a Low-Energy Loser.

Talk about a Low-Energy Loser who contributed to Florida *still* being the laughingstock that it is.

Trust me, I love Florida—I had the most beautiful mansion in Palm Beach—and I have very, very, very successful businesses throughout the Sunshine State.

But that's *despite* Low-Energy Loser Jeb.

Look at his campaign. People fall asleep.

He's boring. He's stupid. His own mother didn't want him to be president—until he decided to run.

Then they told Old Lady Barbara to get with the program, so she backtracked.

But, do you know what?

When Barbara spoke the first time, she was being honest.

And she was right: America has seen *enough* Clintons and *enough* Bushes in the White House!

Now, Barbara—by backtracking—is being a politician who's as phony as Jeb.

So, not only is she a phony, she's a liar.

And is America ready for Jeb in the White House?

Not even his *father* was ready for Jeb and *Jeb's family* to be in the White House!

Do you remember? Do you remember?

Let me remind you.

When George Herbert Walker Bush was president and Jeb was over with his kids, they were, like little kids do, running all over the south lawn with the other little kids.

Then someone asked Bush I which were his grandkids. And he turns to point to the kids and says, "The little brown ones."

The. Little. Brown. Ones.

Yes, that's what Jeb's old man said: *The Little Brown Ones.*

What a racist WASP! What a racist WASP thing to say about your own grandchildren!

That's what he said, that old racist WASP, pointing to his mixed-race grandkids running around like a bunch of little Aztecs at the Pyramid of the Sun outside Mexico City!

And who is Jeb married to?

Who?

He's married to Columba.

A Mexican.

Columba—who can't even speak English without an accent.

Columba, a pre-Columbian relic from a very foreign society.

Is America ready for this? Is America ready for a *Mexican-born* First Lady?

Is America ready for a First Lady who can't speak English without a terrible, terrible accent and will spend her time in the private residence watching *telenovelas* in Spanish on Univision?

Is America ready for pre-Columbian Columba and her Day of the Dead celebrations in the White House?

For Low-Energy Jeb, every day is Day of the Dead, since he acts like he's already dead!

Can you imagine? Can you imagine?

Can you imagine her spending all her time playing patty-cake with that other *Mexican-born* American citizen who can't speak intelligible English: *Jorge Ramos?*

And when the patty-cake session is over and the *telenovela* episode ends in suspense, Jorge Ramos goes back to Univision!

America is not ready for Nightmare on Pennsylvania *Avenida!*

Jeb and his little Aztec offspring! Pre-Columbian Columba and her Virgin of Guadalupe cult!

Do you think that Jeb's Aztec kids will want to build a pyramid on the national Mall?

Leave modern pyramid-building to I. M. Pei at the Louvre!

I. M. Pei! Columba Is Not!

I love Mexico! I really do! And I love the Mexican people! I really do!

Would I want my *daughter* to marry a Mexican?

I have to be honest: No, I wouldn't.

Would I want my *son* to marry a Mexican?

That's a different question.

If the Mexican is Salma Hayek Hot, of course!

Do you hear that, Heidi Klum?

Mexican Salma Hayek is still a Ten! German Heidi Klum is not!

So, yes, I wouldn't mind a Salma Hayek Hot daughter-in-law.

But Columba ranks down there with Hillary Hippo Hips Hypocrite, maybe even less when you consider that pre-Columbian Columba has the blood of Aztec savages running through her veins.

I wouldn't want to see an obsidian knife in *her* hands!

And I wouldn't want to see Low-Energy Loser Jeb in the White House.

Why?

28

Because he's a man of no conviction and he doesn't know his own mind.

Remember when he was asked if he thought his brother's invasion of Iraq was a mistake?

He didn't know what to say!

Of course it was a mistake.

Look, Saddam Hussein was a dictator, but he kept Iraq together and stable. We can't solve the world's problems.

But we went in! We invaded Iraq and we destroyed that country.

Colin Powell was right about that. Remember what General Powell said?

He said, "We break it, we own it."

We broke Iraq, and it's a nightmare that we own: Instability! Al Qaeda! ISIS!

And now, Iran is taking over. And it's costing us billions and billions of dollars without end!

And Jeb is afraid to say it was a mistake because it might hurt his Loser Brother's feelings?

Who cares about W?

Jeb should care about America!

I mean, we spent $2.5 trillion in Iraq. We lost thousands of lives in Iraq. We have wounded warriors, whom I love, all over this country, right?

Was it worth it?

No!

We have *nothing!*

We have nothing over there. His brother made a horrible decision, and Obama made a horrible decision the way America left.

When America left, we should have taken the oil instead of giving it to ISIS and Iran.

And you know who the primary beneficiary—the *only* beneficiary—of the oil is?

China.

China is taking out so much oil that it's a national security threat! It is!

I'm on record having said we shouldn't have gone in, but once we went into Iraq, never, in a million years, should we have left without the oil.

I mean, if you are stupid enough to make the mistake of going in, then, at the very least, you need to have an exit strategy: Take the oil!

If you look at the mess in Iraq today—the rise of ISIS, Iran's takeover of Baghdad—Bush II was an idiot!

Dick Cheney was an idiot!

We never won. We never won in Iraq.

Iraq was a mistake, and until we admit to ourselves this fundamental truth, we're not going to straighten out that mess.

I heard Low-Energy Jeb talking about it. First of all, it took him five days before he could give an answer. And after the pollsters told him what to say, he said it was bad.

Now he's trying to backtrack, probably because his brother said, "Hey, wait a minute, you're killing me here. You said it's bad. That's my legacy, the Iraq War."

The Iraq War is a disaster for the Bushes. *That's* why the last thing we need is another Bush, believe me.

We have ISIS instead of Saddam Hussein.

So, you tell me, was it worth what we paid to have this disaster?

And Jeb, Low-Energy Loser that he is, is limping around the country, trying to pretend he can be president.

Is America ready for a president, living in the White House, who dives into Mexican pussy?

Give *me* break! Give *America* a break!

He *won't* be president. He *can't* be president.

His only hope is if every Latino—many of whom are illegal and can't vote—will vote for him anyway.

And he speaks Spanish on the campaign trail?

Spanish?

That's how this pathetic Low-Energy Loser is campaigning?

Well, I think that when you get right down to it, we are a nation that speaks English. And I think while we're in this nation, we should be speaking English!

Whether people—pre-Columbian Columba included—like it or not, that's how we assimilate.

And I'm not just talking about Spanish. I'm talking about from various parts of the world. That's how they will become successful and do great. So I think it's more appropriate to be speaking English.

So, why am I not afraid of Low-Energy Jeb?

Would you be?

And Jeb Low-Energy Loser is a liar.

Remember?

Do you remember when he said he had "a lot of really cool things" he could be doing instead of running for president?

Who is he kidding?

We all know he doesn't have any cool things to do in his life.

He's the least cool person in America. And it's not surprising! I mean, look at the people around him.

There's Ana Navarro, who's from Nicaragua, talking away on CNN.

Another fat pig Latina blathering away for hours on CNN. It's obvious she's overindulging in *sopa de mondongo,* a Nicaraguan so-called delicacy—which, by the way, is *peasant slop*—from Masatepe, Ground Zero for Nicaraguans who balance baskets of fruit on their heads, which includes baskets filled with pig tripe.

Yes, that's what *sopa de mondongo* is: overcooked pig tripe!

Hey, Ana, lay off that slop!

All that tripe is making you trite!

Who knew that fat pig Ana Navarro is Spanish for fat pig Rosie O'Donnell?

Unbelievable!

And she's been talking on CNN about how everything I do is terrible and everything Jeb does in wonderful.

But who can believe her? If fat pig Ana Navarro is stuffing her face with pig tripe, isn't that a form of cannibalism?

And she talks nonsense!

Guess what?

I'm leading!

Low-Energy Jeb is tanking!

Keep talking, Ana Navarro, because the more you run that fat pig mouth of yours filled with pig tripe on CNN, the more Low-Energy Jeb's number tank!

He's now down in the single digits—and that's with more than $100 million in the bank!

Don't shut up, Ana Navarro!

The more you talk, the more people run away from Low-Energy Jeb once they realize that if—*God forbid*—he should be president, then the nation will be tortured by the sight of your fat pig face blathering away on CNN for four years!

Remember? Remember?

When the campaign started, Low-Energy Jeb was at 16 percent—and after months of Ana Diarrhea-of-the-Mouth Navarro blathering on, Low-Energy Jeb is at 4 percent!

She thinks she's helping him?

Give *me* a break! Give *America* a break!

And can you imagine Ana Navarro on *CNN en Español?*

Talking bullshit in two languages!

But no matter what language you're speaking, when Carly Fiorina comes up, the word is LOSER!

Carly was a little nasty to me—be *careful*, Carly! Be *careful!*

But I can't say anything to her because she's a woman. I *promised* that I wouldn't say that she ran Hewlett-Packard into the ground. I said I wouldn't say it!

That her stock value tanked.

That she laid off tens of thousands of people. That she got viciously fired.

I said I will not *say* that. And that she then went out and ran against Barbara *Boxer,* and lost in a landslide.

She lost against Barbara Boxer—which, by the way, is incredible, since Barbara Boxer is a loser!

How does that even happen?

I know!

Carly is an even bigger LOSER!

And I said, "I. Will. Not. Say. That!"

But she's a Loser!

I'm not saying anything about her impressive track record of failure after failure.

I don't have to: It's all on Google!

In fact, even feminists know she's scary!

I have it right here!

Erin Gloria Ryan, who is the managing editor of the feminist blog Jezebel—can you believe we're reached a point in this country where stupid things like blogs have managing editors?—but this is what she tweeted on Twitter: "Carly Fiorina is an ice-cold shade queen debate princess and I'm in love with and terrified of her."

Feminists are afraid of her!

That's understandable, she's such a LOSER!

And, like Hillary, Carly has bad judgment.

I mean, who is she married to? Mr. Ed?

She sure looks like it!

Look at that face!

Would anyone *vote* for that? Can you imagine that, the face of our next *president*?

I mean, she's a woman, and I'm not supposed say bad things, but really, folks, come on. Are we *serious?*

And I'm not being sexist or guilty of "lookism."

Why?

Because we have a big problem in this country.

The same way that Jeb gets away with being the Low-Energy Loser who flip-flops—or as his father, George Herbert Walker Bush liked to say, "waffles"—over whether or not he agrees that his brother's terrible, terrible invasion of Iraq was a success or a failure, there's something wrong with Carly that a professional stylist can't fix—even if the professional stylist is also a plastic surgeon.

I'm not Brad Pitt, okay?

I know that—and I'm sure Angelina Jolie would never mistake me for her husband!

But I have sense enough to take people's advice on how to look as good as I can.

Why can't Carly do the same thing?

God knows Hillary Hippo Hips Hypocrite shuns the idea of looking good as much a bull dyke with spiked hair, combat boots, and a ring through her nose wants to look human!

But if you want to be in the White House, you have to try—try—*just try*—to look good.

Carly Fiorina reminds of that other horse-faced idiot, Sarah Jessica Parker!

Talk about a woman with terrible, terrible, terrible looks.

Let's face it: Everyone thought *Sex in the City* was science fiction because Sarah Jessica Parker is so ugly.

Sarah Jessica Parker could attract Mr. Big?

Not on this planet!

Look who that horse-face loser is married to? The Pillsbury Doughboy, Matthew Broderick!

But when you have the face of a horse . . .

And that's not me saying it!

Way back in 2007, *Maxim* magazine, which reflects the opinions of American men like no other magazine does, held a poll.

They asked: "Who was the ugliest, ugliest, ugliest female celebrity in the country?"

Guess who won?

Sarah Jessica Parker was voted the "unsexiest" celebrity in the world.

She was followed Amy Winehouse, no surprise there.

The next two losers were Sarah Oh, that scary actress in *Grey's Anatomy*, and then it was Madonna, who looks more like a harpy with each passing hour.

That's not *me* saying Sarah Jessica Parker looks like a horse. That's the Silent *Majority* of American men who voted in the *Maxim* survey casting their votes!

So, if horse-faced Sarah Jessica Parker is the unsexiest celebrity in America, then Carly Fiorina gives her a run for her money.

And ugly is stupid if you have millions in the bank!

How stupid?

Carly, whose terrible, terrible, terrible leadership ruined Hewlett-Packard—although you didn't hear that from me—looks like someone who has no sense when it comes to hiring a personal stylist to make her look good.

What does that make her if not a total loser?

All you have to do is ask any of the thousands and thousands of Hewlett-Packard employees who lost their jobs!

Can you imagine the *millions and millions* of jobs that would be destroyed, destroyed, destroyed if she's elected?

This is why America the Great is America the Mess: too many *Losers* pretending to be *Leaders*.

Jeb in Florida with his pre-Columbian baggage. Carly at Hewlett-Packard with Mr. Ed by her side.

Give *me* a break! Give *America* a break!

Give us all a break from Losers!

Make America Great Again!

Vote Trump.

4. How to Fix Our Broken Immigration System

Our leaders are stupid!

Our borders are out of control.

The last time there was a serious attempt to fix our broken immigration system was when Ronald Reagan was in office.

Ronald Reagan—who, by the way, started out as a Democrat until his views evolved and he became a Republican, my very same journey—was serious about getting control of our borders.

I will follow in the steps of Ronald Reagan—because let's be honest, Bush I did nothing, Clinton in two terms did nothing, Bush II failed to do anything to get immigration under control even after our homeland was attacked on 9/11, and Obama has been a joke, an absolute joke.

I will follow in the steps of Ronald Reagan and, as his conservative heir, I will get immigration under control!

We are led by very stupid, stupid people who don't know how to protect us.

Mexico, for instance, is sending people that have lots of problems, and they are bringing those problems to us.

They are bringing drugs, and bringing crime, and they're rapists.

I have been criticized for saying this, but it's a fact!

I'm going to quote the conclusions of a comprehensive report from the Washington Office of Latin America, known as WOLA, an NGO that has studied this problem very, very carefully.

WOLA concludes: "The stunning frequency of kidnapping, extortion, human trafficking, rape, and homicide puts Central American migrants' plight in Mexico atop the list of the Western Hemisphere's worst humanitarian emergencies."

Kidnapping. Exortion. Human trafficking. Rape. Homicide. These aren't *my* words!

These are the words of an organization that does nothing, nothing, nothing but study this problem!

These are the people that are coming *into* the U.S. *from* Mexico: kidnappers, extortionists, human traffickers, rapists, and killers.

I assume some of the people are good people.

Believe me, I love the Mexican people. I have thousands of Hispanics working for me. They all love me.

Why?

Because I love them because they are good people, good workers. And I treat them well. And they love me because I am fair and deal with them correctly.

But when it comes to immigration, we have to get tough.

Low-Energy Loser —*Jeb*—thinks these people breaking a law when they break into our country do it *out of love* . . .

Did you know that's what Low-Energy Loser Jeb said?

He said, "Yeah, they broke the law, but it's not a felony. It's an act of love."

Give *me* a break! Give *America* a break!

That's like saying Charles Manson broke the law and killed Sharon Tate—who was pregnant, by the way—but it was an act of love!

Low-Energy Loser Jeb is stupid, stupid, stupid!

Love? Forget love, it's time to get tough!

Tough love!

It's time to take back our borders!

Do I think Jeb hates America when he wants to do nothing, nothing, nothing to secure our country's borders?

No, I mean, in all honesty, if my wife were from Mexico, I think I would have a soft spot for people from Mexico.

So I understand that Low-Energy Loser Jeb, who's spent his entire married life eating Mexican pussy, wants more Mexican pussy to come over the border—legal, illegal, anyway he can get more Mexican pussy!

But wanting to eat Mexican pussy is not an immigration policy!

It's a fetish, Okay?

A Trump Immigration Policy—T.I.P.—puts America and the American people *first!*

Not the priorities of Low-Energy Loser governor from Florida and his fetish desire for more Mexican pussy!

Real immigration reform puts the needs of working people first! We are the only country in the world whose immigration system puts the needs of other nations ahead of our own. That must change.

Here are the three core principles of real immigration reform:

1. A nation without borders is not a nation. There must be a wall across the southern border to stop Mexico from sending people that have lots of problems.

2. A nation without laws is not a nation. Laws passed in accordance with our constitutional system of government must be enforced because there's great danger with illegals.

3. A nation that does not serve its own citizens is not a nation. Any immigration plan must improve jobs, wages, and security for all Americans.

This is how we can move forward!

This is what Ronald Reagan would do!

This is how Ronald Reagan, who, by the way, was happy to eat American pussy—not Nancy's, of course—would fix our broken immigration system!

Believe me! Believe me!

I would get our out-of-control immigration under control!

And the first thing I would do is put an end to "anchor" babies: pregnant foreigners sneaking into the U.S. just to give birth so their babies are automatic American citizens.

If a pregnant American mother is traveling to Egypt on business and goes into delivery, do we instantly declare her child an Egyptian?

Of course not!

Four million anchor babies are now officially U.S. citizens.

This has to stop.

This Trump in the White House will *stop* it!

The only other major country in the world that issues citizenship based on where one's mother delivers her child is Canada.

We cannot be like Canada! God help us if we ever became like the lame Canadians!

Why anchor babies?

Welfare payments!

This is one of the consequences—the unintended consequences—of those stupid, stupid, stupid liberals who champion sanctuary cities!

If you announce that you will give sanctuary—*and welfare benefits*—to illegals who happen to be pregnant, guess what?

Pregnant illegals make their way to America just before they are ready to give birth!

This is crazy!

But this is precisely what goes on every day in America: Women who have *zero* connection to the United States cross the border, deliver a baby, and their kid magically becomes an American citizen eligible to receive all the rights and benefits of those who have lived, worked, and paid taxes in our country.

Day 1 in office, I will order my staff to look into ending this!

I will order my staff to look how to reinterpret the Fourteenth Amendment to stop anchor babies.

I understand the Fourteenth Amendment was needed to ensure that former slaves were not denied citizenship—slavery, by the way, was a terrible, terrible idea because it's not a sustainable business model—but that same amendment is now being used to wreak havoc.

The Fourteenth Amendment was never intended to confer citizenship upon the children of illegals born in the U.S.

Do you know what that amendment says?

I have it here!

It reads, "All citizens born or naturalized in the United States, and subject to the jurisdiction thereof, are citizens of the United

States and the state wherein they reside."

Legal scholars—top-rate legal scholars, by the way, not Loser Latino apologist quasi-legal scholars—agree with me when I say that it is the clear purpose of the Fourteenth Amendment, ratified in 1868, three years after the end of the Civil War, to guarantee full citizenship rights to now emancipated former slaves.

That's it!

It was not intended to guarantee illegal immigration to the United States!

We are a nation of laws!

This Trump in the White House will make sure that our immigration policy is rational, fair, compassionate—and *enforced!*

America will only be great as long as America remains a nation of laws that lives according to the Constitution.

No one is above the law.

Now, some of the stupid, stupid, stupid—and I mean *really* stupid—people in the media accuse me of not having specifics.

Well, I do!

The following steps will return to the American people the safety of their laws, which politicians have stolen from them:

Triple the number of ICE officers. Don't take my word for it! Listen to the president of the ICE Officers' Council's explanation when he testified to Congress: "Only approximately 5,000 officers and agents within ICE perform the lion's share of ICE's immigration mission. . . . Compare that to the Los Angeles Police Department at approximately 10,000 officers. Approximately 5,000 officers in ICE

cover 50 states, Puerto Rico and Guam, and are attempting to enforce immigration law against 11 million illegal aliens already in the interior of the United States. Since 9/11, the U.S. Border Patrol has tripled in size, while ICE's immigration enforcement arm, Enforcement and Removal Operations (ERO), has remained at relatively the same size." This initiative will be funded when we accept the recommendations of the Inspector General for Tax Administration and eliminate tax credit payments to illegal

40

immigrants.

Nationwide e-verify. This is a very, very, very simple measure that will protect jobs for unemployed Americans.

Mandatory return of all criminal aliens. The corrupt and depraved Obama White House has released more 76,000 aliens with criminal records into the general population since 2013 alone. Under a Trump administration, all criminal aliens will be returned to their home countries. This is a process which will be aided when we cancel any visas to foreign countries that refuse to accept their own criminal nationals. We will also make it a separate and additional crime to commit an offense while in the U.S. as an illegal.

Detention—not catch-and-release. Illegal aliens that are apprehended crossing the border will be detained and then they will be sent home. This catch-and-release bullshit game ends!

Defund Sanctuary Cities. We will cut off all federal grants to any city which refuses to cooperate with federal law enforcement, part of our ending of these so-called sanctuary cities that harbor alien criminals.

Enhanced penalties for overstaying a visa. Millions of people come to the United States on temporary visas but refuse to leave once their visas expire. They often do this without consequence. This is a threat to national security. Any foreign alien who refuses to leave at the time their visa expires will be subject to criminal penalties. We will also help give local jurisdictions by giving them the authority to hold visa overstays until federal authorities arrive. Completion of a visa tracking system—required by current law but blocked by special interest lobbyists—will be necessary as well.

Cooperate with local gang task forces. ICE officers will accompany local police departments when they conduct raids of violent street gangs like MS-13 and the 18th Street Gang. Gangs terrorize the country and many, many gangs are made up of illegal aliens. In fact, all illegal aliens in gangs will be apprehended and deported. This is how Chris Crane describes the situation: "ICE Officers and Agents are forced to apply the Deferred Action for

Childhood Arrivals (DACA) Directive, not to children in schools, but to adult inmates in jails. If an illegal-alien inmate simply claims eligibility, ICE is forced to release the alien back into the community. This includes serious criminals who have committed felonies, who have assaulted officers, and who prey on children. . . . ICE officers should be required to place detainers on every illegal alien they encounter in jails and prisons, since these aliens not only violated immigration laws, but then went on to engage in activities that led to their arrest by police; ICE officers should be required to issue Notices to Appear to all illegal aliens with criminal convictions, DUI convictions, or a gang affiliation; ICE should be working with any state or local drug or gang task force that asks for such assistance."

End birthright citizenship. This is the biggest magnet for illegal immigration, allowing them to have anchor babies that become a burden on the American taxpayer. By a 2-to-1 margin, voters agree with me that this policy is wrong. This includes none other than Harry Reid—who, by the way, is one week from having to wear adult Depends and having an aide wipe drool from his mouth, if you want to know the truth—who said "no sane country" would give automatic citizenship to the children of illegal immigrants.

There!

Is that a plan with specific policy action items, or what?

All these loser pundits on television—and they *are* loser pundits—forget that I am a very, very, very successful businessman visionary and a visionary businessman.

I would not have billions and billions of dollars in wealth if I didn't know how to make great deals, fantastic deals, unbelievable deals!

And to make great, fantastic, and unbelievable deals you need to have comprehensive, coherent, and successful contracts.

I promise you one thing: I will assemble a fantastic team of competent people to get things done!

George Herbert Walker Bush didn't do it. William Jefferson Clinton didn't do it! George W. Bush didn't do it!

Barack Obama? That Kenyan Socialist wasn't interested in doing it!

His father was from Kenya, and I'll bet his father was never in this country legally. Obama claims to have been born in Hawaii?

Hawaii?

Give *me* a break! Give *America* a break!

Hawaii is closer to *Japan* than it is to *California!*

But anyway, who cares?

Ronald Reagan liked me and I liked him. I want to have that great conservative, great leader, and great president President Ronald Reagan look down on America and be proud that after Bush I, Clinton, Bush II, and Obama we are finally, finally, finally getting our borders under control!

When it comes to our nation's immigration policy, it is time to put an end to a lawless border with Mexico where kidnappers, extortionists, human traffickers, rapists, and killers are allowed to come in as if they belonged here!

And do you know what?

Hispanics love this idea! Latinos love this plan!

Why?

Because the same Loser Leftists that champion sanctuary cities... are the same white liberals who don't know how to *empathize* with Hispanics and Latinos who are in this country legally!

They are so concerned about the rights of *illegals* that they forget about the rights of Hispanics and Latinos in America *legally!*

Let me be clear: Hispanics in America live under a "Cloud of Suspicion" every single day of their lives!

"Is so-and-so legal?" people wonder. "Is so-and-so illegal?" others ask.

How would you feel to live like this, under this "Cloud of Suspicion" every single day.

Well, let me tell you!

Day 1 in office, the illegals begin to be deported!

They have got to go!

And then, when the ILLEGALS are gone, everyone will know that everyone *here* in America has a *right* to be in America!

My immigration plan lifts the "Cloud of Suspicion" that is a burden on the millions of *legal* Hispanics and *legal* Latinos in this country!

Believe me, I have thousands of Hispanics working for me, and I know how much they resent the "Cloud of Suspicion" that is an emotional burden, a source of stress, and a stigma that makes them feel like second-class citizens.

I'm really, really rich because I can empathize with people! I can understand how painful it must be to live under this "Cloud of Suspicion" — which is why I will put an end to it!

Liberal Losers don't know how to empathize with the *legal* Hispanics and the *legal* Latinos in this great country of ours!

They only care about the lawbreakers, not the law abiding!

The possibility that another Bush — Low-Energy Loser Jeb — or another Clinton — Hillary Hippo Hips Hypocrite — becomes president!

The horror! The horror! The horror!

It's something out of *Heart of Darkness*, that's how horrible that idea is!

No more Bushes! No more Clintons!

The Bushes and the Clintons have done enough to destroy America!

Low-Energy Loser Jeb? Hillary Hippo Hips Hypocrite?

Give *me* a break! Give *America* a break!

We need to get our borders under control!

We want a great, wonderful, excellent immigration system that will welcome all the right kinds of immigrants!

Trust me, the economy will be growing so much we will be in desperate need of great people! And we will get great people!

We want great people! We want people of achievement! We need a great, wonderful, and excellent immigration system that will expedite the legal immigration of great people of accomplishment and achievement from the world over!

It's immigration, stupid!

This Trump in the White House would make Ronald Reagan *proud!*

We need a Deportation Force so we can have a kinder, gentler, and great new version of "Operation Wetback."

I really, really, really like Ike!

Make America Great Again!

Vote Trump.

5. Why I Will Stop Iran

Our leaders are stupid!

Our country enters into deals negotiated by stupid, stupid—and I mean very stupid—negotiators.

I'm rich. I'm really, really rich.

And I got that rich by being good at deals. So I've been doing deals for a long time. And the deals have been something!

I've been making lots of wonderful deals, great deals. That's what I do. Never, ever, ever in my life have I seen any transaction so incompetently negotiated as our deal with Iran.

And I mean never.

Why?

Because a successful deal is negotiated from strength—and smarts.

Now, do I think Barack Obama and John Kerry are weak—or stupid?

Maybe they're not bright. I mean I've watched Kerry negotiating. I've asked people, "Is he bright? Is he an intelligent man?"

Maybe they're not bright. Maybe there's something wrong with them. As an example, why say 24 days about inspections?

When we call inspections, we have the right—if not the obligation—to go in immediately.

They didn't negotiate from a position of strength or with great intelligence.

How would you like to be Israel right now?

They relied on us.

We let Israel down. Israel is a voice of sanity. The Israelis, they're great people—and great, reliable, true allies.

And we have a deal that is so incompetent, so bad.

Think of the deal.

Forget the Kenyan Socialist in the Oval Office. Forget him for a moment.

What about John Kerry?

Think about it! Think about it, America!

We are making a deal, and our chief negotiator goes into a bicycle race at 73 years of age. The idiot falls and he breaks his leg. That was the good part of our deal, that our chief negotiator is in the hospital getting operated on his 73-year-old leg!

Is that sound judgment?

That's like Hillary wearing blue pantsuits that make her look like a giant, fat blue robin and brings more attention to her Hippo Hips!

John Kerry's an old, stupid man to think he can be in a bicycle race while negotiating with the Islamic Republic of Iranian Terrorists!

Is he kidding me? Is he kidding America?

And there he is, struggling to get out of a limo here and limo there with his aides fumbling with his crutches as the old fool limps around while, back in Iran, they're getting ready to go atomic!

I swear to you that, as president, I will never, ever ride a bicycle, at least in a race, but I won't ride one anyway.

Would you be surprised if I told you that, on Twitter, Iranian officials were joking about John Kerry and his crutches?

They don't speak Arabic in Iran; they speak Farsi.

And in *Farsi*, all they joked about was the *farce* of the American negotiating delegate!

"Perhaps we should spill a barrel of oil in Mr. Kerry's path, and watch him slip off his crutches!" the Iranian terrorist negotiators were joking.

They wanted John Kerry to slip and have that crutch fly up his ass!

And as these clowns run foreign policy—by the way, if you think John Kerry is a joke as secretary of state, let me remind you that Hillary Hippo Hip Hypocrite was worse—we are being laughed at by everybody!

And I mean *everybody!*

So, with this terrible, terrible deal, what's going to happen?

I think everybody's going to arm. I think it's a disastrous deal, an incompetently done deal.

How bad is it?

Listen to this: We don't even get our four people back.

Did you know that?

Did you know that Iran is holding four Americans hostage? We get nothing. We get nothing.

Why?

I think that John Crutches Boy Kerry has terrible, terrible people, incompetent people, working for him.

It's a disgrace!

We should have doubled up the sanctions, and we should have made a deal with more intelligence.

It's no secret that Obama rushed this deal so he would have a legacy.

I know, you know, we all know what little he has accomplished in these two terms, so he's *desperate* to get a deal—*any deal*—just to get a *deal!*

We were negotiating out of desperation. We look so desperate, and it's a disgrace.

I think the deal is absolutely something out of a horror show.

Don't get me wrong. I love the idea of a deal. But this deal is a horror deal!

It's not a well-negotiated deal, this terrible Iran deal. We should have doubled up the sanctions and made a much better deal.

Day 1 in office, the Iran deal is done.

And the message to the ayatollahs is that American strength is back.

Now, it's true that Iranians got, a couple of years ago, one of their nuclear scientists back.

What did we get?

We got nothing. The theory was we didn't get our hostages out because it was too *complicated* to ask.

48

Too *complicated?* Are you kidding me?

They didn't read *The Art of the Deal*—which, by the way, was a worldwide best-seller.

They didn't think to say, "Fellows, give us our prisoners back."

That's not too complicated.

Remember Jimmy Carter?

Let me tell you this about Jimmy Carter.

Jimmy Carter is a good man, a Christian man. What he has done with Habitat for Humanity and all the other good works is wonderful.

But, as president, he was terrible, terrible, absolutely terrible!

Our hostages were held in Iran for 444 days.

Remember that?

And do you remember when they were released?

Our hostages left Iranian air space—*to come back to America*—on the day Ronald Reagan was inaugurated.

Why?

I'll tell you why.

Because the ayatollahs knew Carter was weak and wouldn't do anything, but that Reagan was going to kick their asses!

The ayatollahs knew Reagan was strong, and they didn't want to fuck with the Old Gipper.

Now, Jimmy Carter is sick and, God bless him, I wish him success fighting cancer. And do you know what he says?

I have it right here.

Jimmy Carter has one regret about the Iranian hostage crisis: "I wish I had sent one more helicopter to get the hostages, and we would've rescued them, and I would've been reelected."

Those savages only understand strength. And Obama has not shown strength.

Remember Obama and his famous "red lines" that can't be crossed?

Well, guess what, the Russians crossed that red line in Ukraine—and we have done nothing. And the year before that, in 2013, Syrian

President Bashar al-Assad, who is a terrible tyrant controlled by the Russians, by the way, crossed the red line that Obama set.

And America did nothing.

We are led by stupid, stupid people—very, very stupid people.

Do you know what has happened as a result our leaders' stupidity?

Four years of civil war in Syria—and half, think of it—*half* of all Syrians are now refugees!

Because of Hillary Hippo Hips Hypocrite and John Crutches-Boy Kerry we have no credibility.

That's happened while we had LOSERS for secretaries of state: Hillary Hippo Hips Hypocrite and John Crutches-Boy Kerry!

And now, Europe has the worst refugee crisis since World War II.

"You're welcome, Europe!"

Europe was *stupid* enough to give Obama a Nobel Peace Prize before he did anything, and this is how Obama repays Europe, with half of Syria's people to take in as refugees!

"You're welcome, Europe!"

We failed to follow through with military action once red lines were crossed, and we undermined our credibility in negotiating with the Islamic Republic of Iranian Terrorists!

Remember what Reagan said about war?

He said, "Of the four wars in my lifetime, none came about because the U.S. was too strong."

Think about that!

Under Obama, we are weak.

Just ask the people in Ukraine, who have been abandoned after the Russians crossed the meaningless, meaningless "red line." Just ask half of the people of Syria—*half of that nation has fled war*—about the bullshit promises to do something if that Syrian dictator crossed the meaningless, meaningless "red line."

Because we are weak and we don't keep our word, that's why the ayatollah suckered us.

50

They have taken advantage of stupid people, stupid negotiators, people that are incompetent, whether it's John Crutches-Boy Kerry, or the Kenyan Socialist in the Oval Office.

Let me tell you something, so listen up!

If I win the presidency, I guarantee you that those four prisoners are back in our country before I ever take office.

They will be back before I ever take office because the Iranians know that's what has to happen!

They know it. And if they don't know it, I'm telling them right now.

Remember, I make the best deals in the world because I'm the best negotiator in the world!

I'm a delegator! I find absolutely great people!

There's no room for Hillary Hippo Hips Hypocrite or John Crutches-Boy Kerry, two terrible, terrible losers who have done more harm to America than I want to even think about!

Let me tell you something else!

We will have so much winning if I get elected that you may get bored with winning. Believe me when I say you'll never get bored with winning.

We never get bored with winning, believe me on that!

So Iran got the best of us because we ended up with a terrible, terrible deal.

America is tired of Bush I, Clinton, Bush II, and Obama.

Why?

Because everything is talk in this country. They talk and talk.

And the result?

We end up with a ridiculous deal. Even a thing like, you know, stopping nuclear proliferation, is taken as a joke by Hillary Hippo Hips Hypocrite and John Crutches-Boy Kerry.

Stopping nuclear proliferation is so important.

You wouldn't know it by looking at what our stupid, stupid leaders are doing.

You may not know it, but while this terrible, terrible deal—

which, by the way, is a betrayal of our commitment to our friend and ally, Israel—the ayatollah is holding Americans as prisoners.

"Hostages" is more like it!

At the beginning of these so-called "negotiations," they had three prisoners, and they now have four prisoners.

It didn't occur to our leaders to include the release of Americans held hostage in the Islamic Republic of Iranian Terrorists in the deal?

We are weak!

We are Jimmy Carter–weak!

We need to be Ronald Reagan–strong!

Remember how Ronald Reagan brought down the Berlin Wall?

Remember his words: "Here's my strategy on the Cold War: We win, they lose."

American can never be a great country again if we continue to lose!

We make a deal with Iran, and Iran is *still* holding four American hostages?

Automatically you say, Listen, it's not going to do you any good, release the prisoners!

That would send a great signal to everybody.

John Crutches-Boy spoke about making a deal with Iran while Iran is holding Americans.

Do you know what that stupid, stupid secretary of state, who, by the way, believe it or not, is as stupid as Hillary when she was at the State Department, said about it?

He said, "One thing has nothing to do with the other."

Give *me* a break! Give *America* a break!

And, to make matters worse, we don't get our hostages back but Iran gets BILLIONS!

This Iran deal gives billions and billions of dollars to the ayatollahs, releasing the money before you even do the deal where they're getting billions of dollars, they are going to be so rich and so powerful.

And, you know, when you talk about the deal itself, anytime, anywhere, you have to go in and inspect anytime, anywhere. Now, they have a 24-day notice provision.

Give a 24-day notice to go in and inspect?

Are we crazy or just stupid crazy?

I promise you this: Our four hostages will be on their way to American soil before I take the oath of office!

Why?

Because the ayatollahs will know that American weakness ends on Day 1 of a Trump administration!

If I win the election, I will send a message to Iran.

It will be a photograph of Hiroshima after we detonated an atomic bomb over that city to end World War II.

And I will send them the coordinates of Tehran:

Do you know what they are?

Latitude: 35° 41' 39" N

Longitude: 51° 25 17" E

I'm sure those rag-head ayatollahs can put the picture of Hiroshima after we went atomic on Japan and GPS coordinates together and know what I mean: Death to America?

How about a hydrogen bomb over Tehran, you fucking Medieval Age theocratic losers?

That's my message to the Islamic Republic of Iranian Terrorists.

Negotiate a fake deal that gives Iran billions and billions of dollars while the ayatollah is holding four Americans hostage?

Do you know how we ended up with this terrible, terrible deal?

Because we are weak. And because we caved in to Iran, a nation strangled by insanity and intolerance.

They don't have wine! They don't have bacon!

The same insanity and intolerance that characterizes Iran also threatens America!

Melissa Click! She's a Nazi who tried to stifle free speech.

Remember? Remember?

She's the Nazi bully who asked for "muscle" to bully a reporter.

"Hey, who wants to help me get this reporter out of here! I need some muscle over here!" that American Nazi screamed.

That's what it's like in Iran! That's why we have to stop this terrible, terrible Iran deal.

And let me tell you something, a country is either a country or it is not.

We need to enforce our laws. We need to enforce our immigration laws.

Did you know we have Iranian spies in America? We do!

Some have entered on tourist visas. Others have come here on student visas. When they outstay their visas, we do nothing!

I like Ike!

I like the way Ike rounded up illegals and deported them!

He was a great president and I will be a great president. If you liked Ike, then you will love me!

Of course, Low-Energy Loser Jeb opposes me on this.

It's understandable. If we started to deport illegals—whether they're from Iran or Mexico—he's afraid that half of pre-Columbian Columba's family will be sent back. They way Mexicans breed, his extended family must be half a million illegals strong!

And that makes America weak.

It makes America weak the way the Iran deal makes America weak.

And I will stop this terrible, terrible Iran deal!

Give *me* a break! Give *America* a break!

I have eight words for the ayatollah: *We nuked Hiroshima—and we will nuke Tehran!*

Israel will back us on this! Half of Syria's population, fleeing civil war and ISIS, will back us on this!

Everyone on this planet against terrorism will back us on this!

This Trump in the White House will make America safe from the threat of an Islamic Republic of Iranian Terrorists getting an atomic weapon!

Make America Great Again!

Vote Trump.

6. We Must Stop Bad Trade Deals

Our leaders are stupid!

Our economy is being destroyed by trade deals that are terrible—terrible for the American economy and the American people.

Look, I've made billions and billions of dollars by making great deals, terrific deals, world-class deals.

It's true—no one running for president knows the art of the deal like I do. I literally wrote the book, *The Art of the Deal*.

No one else can say that.

No one else can say that he or she—being deferential to horse-faced Carly Fiorina, who, by way, almost destroyed Hewlett-Packard single-handedly—wrote the global best-seller *The Art of the Deal*.

And the art of deal-making, world-class deal making is that you have to get something out of the deal.

Do you remember back in the 1990s when President George Herbert Walker Bush—Bush I—was negotiating the North American Free Trade Agreement—NAFTA?

They didn't ask me what I thought, but I told them what I thought.

I thought it was terrible.

But did Bush I listen?

No, he went on and negotiated with Canada and Mexico to create this terrible, terrible deal that has cost millions and millions of American jobs.

NAFTA has made us—I'm not kidding—physically sicker, and created social upheavals throughout the United States, Canada, and Mexico.

And then, in 1994, there's a ceremony. Bush I—who's only slightly less stupid than his son, Bush II—is there with Canada's Loser Prime Minister Brian Mulroney and Mexican President Carlos

Salinas, who, by the way, looks like Speedy González if Speedy González were a thief.

What was this ceremony about?

The Three Amigos celebrated the implementation of NAFTA!

Well, the Three Amigos are, truth be told, the Three ENEMIGOS of the American, Canadian, and Mexican peoples!

Two years before the disastrous, disastrous NAFTA was passed, we were warned.

Remember Ross Perot?

He's an American patriot in whose footsteps, by the way, I wouldn't mind following. Perot warned us about NAFTA.

"The Huge Sucking Sound," Perot said, warning America of the loss of millions and millions of jobs that NAFTA would destroy. In the second 1992 presidential debate, Ross Perot said, and I quote him:

"We have got to stop sending jobs overseas. It's pretty simple: If you're paying $12, $13, $14 an hour for factory workers and you can move your factory south of the border, pay a dollar an hour for labor ... have no health care—that's the most expensive single element in making a car— have no environmental controls, no pollution controls and no retirement, and you don't care about anything but making money, there will be a giant sucking sound going south. . . . When [Mexico's] jobs come up from a dollar an hour to six dollars an hour, and ours go down to six dollars an hour, and then it's leveled again. But in the meantime, you've wrecked the country with these kinds of deals."

That's what Ross Perot said, and Bush I wouldn't hear any of it.

Bush I was eager to ignore Ross Perot—a businessman visionary like I'm a business visionary—and instead, Bush I listened to idiots.

Idiota Número Uno was Gary Hufbauer of the bullshit Institute for International Economics.

This is what Gary Hufbauer said about the first year—*the first year*—if NAFTA were enacted. Imbecile Gary said, "NAFTA will generate a $7 to $9 billion surplus that would ensure the net creation of 170,000 jobs in the U.S. economy the first year."

56

It didn't happen. It didn't happen at all, folks.

He assured us that in 1995, alone, NAFTA would create 170,000 jobs. That's like Hillary Hippo Hips Hypocrite promising New York State she would, as senator, bring 500,000 to the state.

It didn't happen.

In the first year of NAFTA's implementation, the United States *lost* 225,000 jobs!

Ross Perot, in whose footsteps I would be proud to follow, was right:

Huge!

Sucking!

Sound!

NAFTA was a terrible deal years 25 years ago when it was implemented. And over the past quarter century, millions of Americans' jobs have disappeared—to Mexico, to China, to other countries.

The hemorrhaging of jobs began at once.

Whirlpool closed its facilities in Ohio to move their factories to Mexico. There was shock and disbelief when American workers making Maytags found out they were being replaced by Mexican workers 3,000 miles away.

What Whirlpool began back in the late 1990s has continued without anyone—not Clinton, not Bush II, and certainly not Obama, whose birth certificate, by the way, I have never seen—doing anything to stop it.

And there's no end in sight!

Ford is building a $2.5 billion plant in Mexico!

Can you believe it? Can you believe it?

I'll actually give the goddamn economic traitors at the Ford Motor Company a good idea: Why don't we just let the illegals drive the cars and trucks right into our country?

Give *me* a break! Give *America* a break!

If elected, I can promise you that I won't let Ford move jobs to Mexico and will convince Ford CEO Mark Fields to bring jobs back to the United States.

I'll pick up the phone and call him, Mark Fields, that goddamn economic traitor.

I will say the deal is not going to be approved! I won't allow it! I want that plant in the United States, preferably in Detroit!

There is such a thing as economic treason. And Mark Fields is pretty close to committing economic treason against the United States of America!

What if he doesn't move the factory back?

Then, let me give you the bad news for Ford: Every car, every truck, and every part manufactured in this plant that comes across the border, we're going to charge you a 35-percent tax—okay?—and that tax is going to be paid simultaneously with the transaction.

Economic traitor Mark Fields thinks he can just take away thousands of jobs?

Not if there's a President Trump in the White House!

These deals have devastated our country.

That stops when I'm elected. In fact, if the economy grows the way it should grow when I'm elected, if I bring jobs back from China, from Japan, from Mexico, from so many other countries that are taking our jobs! You get them back by taking them away from other countries!

How?

When *fair* trade replaces *free* trade.

The truth is that Mexico is the new China!

And I say that with admiration.

Think about it. With all their problems—and Mexico certainly has many, many problems—Mexico is beating China!

How are they doing it?

I mean, this is a country where they have done nothing, nothing, nothing to stop millions of Mexicans from walking around balancing baskets of fruit on their heads and walking around dressed as if they were going to a Frida Kahlo costume party!

Wake up!

It's the 21ˢᵗ century! Take the basket off your head! Get clothes from The Gap!

But despite its pre-Columbian appearances, Mexico is winning. It's true. They are winning because our leaders are stupid!

You know what? Mexico is making a fortune from us.

Our companies are moving into Mexico more than almost any other place right now. We are losing our industry. We're losing our business to Mexico.

And it's not just manufacturing.

Nabisco.

Yes, Nabisco.

I love Oreos. But I will never eat them again. Nabisco is closing the plant in Chicago and they are moving the plant to Mexico.

Why?

It can't be because it makes sense.

And do you why I know it doesn't make sense? Because *Mexican* bakeries are moving into the U.S.—and taking over.

I'll bet none of the other candidates know that he biggest baker in the world is a *Mexican* company.

Its name is stupid, but it's run by brilliant people.

It's called Bimbo, yeah, what Hillary Hippo Hips Hypocrite called Monica Lewinsky and what anyone with common sense would call Huma Abedin, the Muslim confidant to Hillary, who's such a bimbo she stays married to Jew Perv who lied to her twice about Bing! Bing! Bing! Bong! Bong! Bong!

This company, Bimbo, you may not have heard of them, but you certainly know—*and eat*—their products.

Are you ready, America?

Are you ready to find out what the Mexicans who run Bimbo are making?

Their brands include Thomas' English Muffins. Those muffins aren't English! They're Mexican!

Bimbo makes Sara Lee! Sara Lee is Mexican!

They make Entenmann's! You think they're German—but think

again!

They make Oroweat! Yes, Oroweat!

And the list goes on: Arnold Bread is Mexican. Boboli sounds Italian, but it's Mexican!

This is what NAFTA has done: American companies sending millions of jobs to Mexico and Mexican companies taking over the brands Americans have loved for generations.

Are you ready for more shocking news!

Mexico is so good—because their leaders are so brilliant at taking American jobs, that—guess what?

Mexico is now stealing jobs from *China?*

China!

The Mexicans are beating the Chinese at their own job-stealing game!

Ever hear of Flambeau?

That's an American company that was thinking of moving their factory to China. But just about when they were ready to take their jobs and ship them off to China—Mexico stepped in.

Flambeau is in Mexico!

This company makes yo-yos! A yo-yo company shipped its jobs to Mexico!

Give *me* a break! Give *America* a break!

This has been happening under Clinton, Bush II, and now Obama.

Whirlpool takes its jobs to Mexico. Ford takes its jobs to Mexico. Nabisco thinks Mexicans are better at making Oreos than Americans can make Oreos right here in America.

Even American yo-yos are being made by Mexican workers.

NAFTA has been a disaster for America.

And NAFTA is only one of the terrible, terrible trade deals that our stupid, stupid, stupid leaders have negotiated.

And when I say I know how to make great deals, world-class deals, I say that because I know that a sustainable deal has to be a win-win situation.

Look, it might seem like Mexico came out ahead with NAFTA. And in some ways, it did.

Mexico has taken millions of American jobs. But that doesn't mean that it ends there.

As a businessman visionary, I know—like Steve Jobs knew and like Ross Perot knows—that you have to see the entire picture, the totality of the deal.

The *totality* of the deal takes into consideration *secondary effects* of the deal.

This is what I mean: *Everyone* is worse off because of NAFTA.

With all these millions of jobs that Mexico has been sucking out of the U.S., you'd think they'd be better off.

Guess what?

They're not.

Mexicans are being exploited by their government—and by these opportunistic, unpatriotic companies shipping millions of jobs off to Mexico.

Did you know that the average Mexican works 2,250 hours a year?

The average American works 1,750 hours a year.

Did you know that almost half of Mexicans live in poverty?

Almost 1 in 5 Americans live in poverty.

How does this make sense?

How can Mexicans work *more* hours and live in poverty? How can Americans—*so many Americans*—live in poverty in the greatest, or what used to be the greatest, nation in the world?

Blame NAFTA.

I love Mexico! I love the Mexican people!

That's why I'm outraged that this trade deal is as bad for *them* as it is for *us*.

We, in America, have lost millions of jobs, and it isn't as if Mexico has benefited that much from it.

How can that be the case when, *after a quarter century*, almost half the people in Mexico *still* live in poverty?

But if you think NAFTA can't get worse, it does.

Did you know there's a direct correlation between a bad trade deal and the public's health?

There is!

As soon as NAFTA was enacted, Mexicans came under pressure to work for American companies and adopt a stressful, hectic lifestyle. There were widespread changes in the Mexican diet—away from grains and to processed foods.

McDonald's, Burger King, Kentucky Fried Chicken, Pizza Hut, and all those other companies invaded Mexico.

The result?

Obesity. Heart disease. Diabetes.

When did George Herbert Walk Bush, Brian Mulroney, or Carlos Salinas tell the American, Canadian, or Mexican people that, as soon as NAFTA was implemented, the American, Canadian, and Mexican people would suffer from epidemics?

NEVER!

Mexico is suffering an obesity epidemic, a heart disease epidemic, and a diabetes epidemic.

It's a public health *crisis* more devastating than AIDS!

And not *one* of my opponents identifies *this* as a threat, a public health threat.

Look, thanks to NAFTA, Americans are now the fattest people in the world—and the Mexicans come in second.

Two out of three Americans is obese. Two out of three Mexicans is obese.

There are seven million diabetics in Mexico, causing 70,000 deaths.

There are twenty-six million diabetics in America, resulting in seven million deaths.

Our leaders are stupid not to see the totality of these trade deals!

Mexico is confronting the same NAFTA health crisis that we are!

This has got to stop.

These obesity, heart disease, and diabetes crises have to stop.

The public health crisis ushered in by NAFTA kills more Americans than listening to one of Low-Energy Loser Jeb's speeches!

And these problems don't stop at the border.

Do you know Carlos Quintanilla on MSNBC?

He's that chubby Mexican-American on MSNBC. Sometimes he sits in for the NBC Nightly News—which, by the way, is a terrible, terrible news broadcast.

Well, what does he look like?

He looks like a Mexican-American Doughboy. I mean, you poke that guy with a needle and diabetes spurts out!

Carlos, get a personal trainer! What's your blood sugar level? How do you say "cardiac arrest" in Mexican Spanish?

And have you seen Ruben Navarrette?

He's that obnoxious pseudo-journalist pontificating about everything?

Look, you stick a pin in that fat pig and LARD oozes out like sap from a tree!

It's people like him that are going to bankrupt Obamacare— which, by the way, I will repeal!

Fat pigs!

Good grief! If fat pig Rosie O'Donnell were to pull a Chaz Bono, or become a drag king, she'd look like fat pig Ruben Navarrette!

And, because of NAFTA, the Mexicans are beginning to look like fat pigs!

Why?

Because we are *exporting* obesity to Mexico.

Yes, that's what's happening in Mexico.

Mexicans are becoming fat pigs like Rosie O'Donnell!

Not all of them, of course.

Salma Hayek is still hot. I wouldn't mind her as a daughter-in-law, but most Mexicans?

Do you think that Mexicans are happy when they look in the mirror and they see that fat pig Rosie O'Donnell looking back at them?

Do you think Mexican officials are happy that diabetes and heart disease are bankrupting their health-care system?

Do you think Mexicans are happy to be working like *slaves* for corporate America?

That's what these terrible, terrible trade deals produce: low-wage slaves overseas, and Americans *enslaved* to unemployment and welfare.

The idea that our stupid, stupid, so very stupid leaders have entered into terrible, terrible, so very terrible trade deals is an outrage.

Billions of people are now low-wage slaves to corporate America—in Mexico, in China, in Bangladesh, in India, and in every corner of the world.

And millions and millions of Americans, good, decent Americans, have been thrown onto the streets—millions so discouraged that they no longer are counted as "unemployed" because they have given up looking for work!

As an American, I am outraged! As a Christian, I am outraged.

To think that our stupid, stupid, so very stupid people have enacted terrible, terrible, so very terrible trade deals that are creating a world of low-wage slaves abroad and transforming America into a nation of quitters, people who have given up on a better future!

Look at Mexico!

The plight of the Mexican people—working so hard for so little and coming down with chronic diseases from the stress—these are the *unintended consequences* of NAFTA.

And no one is talking about it—except me, because I know that a deal is not sustainable unless everyone is better off because of it!

America is not better off because of NAFTA. Mexico is not better off because of NAFTA. Canada, I presume, is not better off because of NAFTA, but with the Canadians, it's hard to know if they have a pulse in the first place, that's how fucking boring the Canadians are!

It's true! They are!

Even Alex Trebek! Alex may have gotten American citizenship,

64

but he's still a boring Canadian in America!

Do you think that had there been a referendum people in the U.S. or Mexico would have voted for NAFTA?

Who cares about Canada, a country of eunuchs who go along with whatever their socialist bureaucrats tell them to do?

But in the U.S. or in Mexico?

Do you think that if Bush I had said: "Hey, folks, if you vote for NAFTA millions of American jobs will disappear and Americans will become fat pigs like Rosie O'Donnell," Americans would have said, "That's a great idea! We want to be unemployed fat fucks who look like fat pig Rosie O'Donnell!"

Of course not!

And do you think that if Carlos Salinas had said, "Hey, amigos, if you vote for NAFTA, you'll work hundreds of hours more than Americans, still live in poverty, and you'll blow up like blimps, suffer from diabetes, and look like fat pig *gringa* Rosie O'Donnell—if you don't drop dead from clogged arteries first," the Mexicans would have said, "*¡Sí! ¡Sí! ¡Sí!* Make us slaves to corporate America, give us First World chronic diseases, and make us look like fat pig *gringa* Rosie O'Donnell!"

Of course not!

We've lost our *wealth!* We've lost our *health!*

Bush I was WRONG on trade! Clinton was WRONG on trade! Bush II was WRONG on trade! Obama is a disaster, disaster, disaster on trade!

And the horrors continue!

The Trans-Pacific Partnership trade deal is going to be another huge sucking sound of lost American jobs not just with Canada and Mexico—but with *eleven* Pacific Rim countries!

This deal, which Obama negotiated as part of his grand Kenyan Socialist scheme—which, by the way, Hillary Clinton championed as secretary of state—now ties together 40 percent of the world's economy!

It encompasses countries from Canada to Australia, Japan to

Chile.

Eleven more countries to steal our jobs and fuck us over!

Unbelievable!

It was sold to the American people as a trade pact that would be a bulwark against China's economic might, but what it will do is destroy millions and millions of American jobs!

Give *me* a break! Give *America* a break!

Day 1 in office, this ends!

Day 1 in office, any company that ships an American job overseas, will pay a 35 percent duty when it ships back its products—whether it is an automobile or a yo-yo!

Day 1 in office, all these terrible, terrible trade deals are renegotiated!

Day 1 in office, America and Mexico will work together to end health crises our two nations face because of NAFTA's unintended consequences!

Day 1 in office, we work for win-win trade deals!

We cannot have trade deals where Mexicans are enslaved to corporate American and where Americans are discarded to the unemployment lines!

We cannot have trade deals that make people dead sick with chronic diseases!

We cannot have trade deals that take away the dreams of the American people for a better future!

Twenty-five years into this terrible, terrible experiment we know the answer: *Ross Perot was right and George Herbert Walker Bush was wrong!*

Let me repeat what Ross Perot said: NAFTA IS A DISASTER FOR THE AMERICAN WORKER!

No more Bushes in the White House! Barbara Bush got that one right!

Americans can't afford more Bush trade deals—that are terrible, terrible for our economy and the health of the American people!

President Trump is what the doctor ordered to cure the malady

that is NAFTA!
   Make America Great Again!
   Vote Trump.

7. We Must Fulfill Our Obligations to Our Veterans

Our leaders are stupid!

We think we can walk away from our responsibilities to the men and women who have served in our armed forces.

It's an honor to serve our country, and it's an honor for our nation to provide for those men, women, and intersex persons, who defend us.

Did I serve?

Everyone wants to know that. No, I didn't serve in Vietnam.

The truth is my Vietnam draft number was so incredible, and it was a very high draft number, so I never had to do that, serve in the military. But I felt that I was in the military in the true sense because I dealt with those people.

That doesn't mean that I don't have any military experience. I relish my five years at the military academy and I bemoan now, as I have over the decades, the dwindling enrollment at such schools.

After the Vietnam War, all those military academies lost ground because people really disrespected the military. People weren't sending their kids to military schools. It was a whole different thing, but in those days—I graduated in 1964—that was a very good thing or tough thing, and it was a real way of life at military academy.

But I want to tell you something you know in your heart to be true: *We have to take care of our vets.*

We have to take care of the men, women, and intersex persons who make our freedom possible.

And when we don't take care of our veterans, then we have failed as a nation.

Now, I have been criticized for pointing out that our veterans have been neglected by not only the Obama administration but also by Bush I, Clinton, and Bush II.

In fact, our veterans have been ignored by *other* veterans in a position of authority!

The reality is that John McCain the politician has made America less safe, sent our brave soldiers into wrongheaded foreign misadventures, covered up for Obama with the Veterans Administration scandal, and has spent most of his time in the Senate pushing amnesty for illegals.

The truth is that the Veterans Administration is the most corrupt group of people in all of Washington!

If ISIS took over America, I'd ask them to behead the administrators of the Veterans Administration first!

We have to take care of the men, women, and—yes—intersex persons who served our country.

I promise to take care of our veterans.

God knows everyone else in Washington has failed them!

John McCain, for one, has certainly failed our veterans. He would rather protect the Iraqi border than Arizona's border.

I'm going to say what I have said before: I have respect for Senator McCain.

In fact, I used to like him a lot. I used to support him a lot.

But I would love to see him do a much better job of taking care of our nation's veterans.

It's America's duty!

But McCain didn't do it—and hasn't done it!

Is he a war hero?

He's not a war hero. He *thinks* he's a war hero because he was captured. I like people who weren't captured.

And I like officials to look after our veterans even better!

In fact, for as long as Senator McCain has been in the U.S. Senate, our veterans have been neglected.

He entered the U.S. Senate in 1987—and in those 28 years since he's been in the Senate, the situation for our veterans has deteriorated.

Remember Ron Kovic?

He's the Vietnam vet who wrote *Born on the Fourth of July*. That was published in 1976, our nation's bicentennial.

You'd think that, eleven years later, when John McCain entered the U.S. Senate, he would have taken lessons from Kovic's book to improve the care our veterans receive.

If he was too busy to read the book—which, by the way, tells how Ron Kovic led a 19-day hunger strike at the federal building in downtown Los Angeles to protest the poor treatment veterans were receiving—then Senator McCain might have seen the movie.

Remember?

Born on the Fourth of July was made into a movie in 1989 starring Tom Cruise.

A war drama!

Tom Cruise earned an Academy Award nomination. Oliver Stone cowrote the script with Ron Kovic. It won two Academy Awards.

I don't believe Senator McCain didn't see the movie.

And yet, in the almost three decades that he's been in office, Senator McCain has witnessed the deterioration in the quality of health care that our veterans receive.

That makes him a hero?

Give *me* a break! Give *America* a break!

More importantly, give our *veterans* a *break*—and better health care!

Now, are you ready to hear something shocking?

Are you ready, because it is pretty shocking?

Our Veterans Administration has failed our veterans so terribly, terribly, terribly much that, since the Vietnam War, our veterans, out of frustration, have *left* the United States to get adequate health care.

Remember the movie?

Ron Kovic left the United States and went to Mexico. He moved to a town he calls "the Village in the Sun."

And there, he gets well.

So here's the shocking news: Did you know that thousands upon thousands of American vets have gone to Mexico—and Canada—to get adequate health care?

Did you know that?

I was shocked when I learned that, for four decades, Mexico has been providing health care to American veterans!

But it was there for us to see—Tom Cruise in *Born on the Fourth of July*, going to Mexico to clean himself up and get well.

Outrageous! Outrageous!

Now, I want a show of hands!

How many people believe that American taxpayers should pay for food stamps that illegals in this country get?

Show of hands!

Not one hand is up!

No one believes that American taxpayers should pay for food stamps for illegals.

Now, another show of hands!

How many believe that Mexican taxpayers should pay for our veterans' health care?

Not one hand is up!

No one believes that *Mexican* taxpayers should pay for health care for *American* veterans.

But do you see how the stupid, stupid, stupid people we have in office have made a mess of things?

Here we are, American taxpayers, spending hundreds of millions of dollars in food stamps for illegals and Mexican taxpayers are spending hundreds of millions of dollars in health care for American veterans!

This has got to stop!

If we expect Mexico to take care of its people—which will happen on Day 1 when I start to deport the illegals—then America must take care of our veterans.

And these terrible policies—championed by former war captives who spent the war locked away in a cave like Senator McCain—have wreaked havoc on our veterans.

Thousands upon thousands of American veterans are in Mexico, for the health care.

American veterans in Mexico and Canada must come home!

Those that served our nation should be taken care of *by us* — not Mexico, not Canada!

Our stupid, stupid, so very stupid leaders have allowed the Veterans Administration to provide terrible, terrible, so very terrible medical services to our veterans!

And the incompetence, the sheer stupidity, the moral outrage is so great that there are now organizations stepping in to provide for our veterans.

How many have seen the commercials on television for the Wounded Warriors!

A show of hands!

Everyone!

How can you miss it? It's on television every single day!

Wounded Warriors exists because the Veterans Administration has failed the men and women who have served in our armed forces!

We've become a nation of ingrates — no one cares! It's impossible to turn on television without a commercial for the Wounded Warriors — they are *begging* me to send them $19 dollars a month to help veterans!

What?

With billions squandered on these wars of deceit by the Pentagon, we are reduced to begging for $19 dollars a month from the public to take care of those who fought for our nation in those wars of conquest fabricated from lies! Iraq had nothing to do with September 11! There were never any weapons of mass destruction!

We sent our precious men and women into a stupid, stupid, stupid war in Iraq that has proved to be the worst disaster in this century!

And we have thousands upon thousands of veterans leaving our country to get the health care they need!

This stops!

This stops on Day 1 of the Trump administration!

Day 1 in office, our Veterans Administration is reformed.

Day 1 in office, veterans will not die while waiting to see a doctor.

Day 1 in office, America will take care of the men and women who took care of protecting our freedoms.

Let me tell you something.

We live in a world where the media ignores what is happening around us.

On September 14, I spoke to 20,000 people at the American Airlines Center Arena in Dallas! Sellout crowd! Every seat was taken!

Incredible! Incredible people! It was an incredible event!

And if you look back at the CNN coverage of that event, you'll see that, at the bottom of the screen, it said: "BREAKING NEWS: Trump: My Hair Is Not That Bad."

It's true!

That's what CNN reported as "Breaking News."

My hair is not that bad.

Now do you understand why America thinks CNN is a joke?

My hair is not that bad. But CNN *is* that bad—*and worse!*

I want to meet the idiot, the complete idiot, at CNN who approved that that be broadcast as "Breaking News."

Breaking News?

The media is broken!

The media is filled with stupid, stupid, very stupid people!

And they do a terrible, terrible job of informing the American public!

I'm not a news reporter. I'm a businessman, a real estate developer. I can build things and I can negotiate world-class deals.

But since CNN is too busy with its Breaking News about my hair, I'll take the opportunity to remind you why the Veterans Administration, under this terrible, terrible president we have, has failed our veterans.

In 2012, just three years ago, Dr. Katherine Mitchell, an emergency room physician, warned Sharon Helman, the new director at the Phoenix Veterans Affairs Healthcare System, that the Phoenix Veterans Administration was overwhelmed, that it couldn't handle the number of veterans who needed attention. Later that year, the U.S. Department of Veterans Affairs ordered implementation of electronic wait-time tracking and made improved patient access a top priority to address the long wait times.

Obama called the situation "intolerable" and "disgraceful."

Then he went to play golf.

In March 2013, Debra Draper, of the General Administration Office, testified to a House subcommittee that, and I quote, "Although access to timely medical appointments is critical to ensuring that veterans obtain needed medical care, long wait times and inadequate scheduling processes at VAMCs medical centers have been persistent problems."

VAMCs are Veteran Administrations Medical Centers.

Obama called the situation "intolerable" and "disgraceful."

Then he went to play golf.

Four months later, there was an email—*here we go again with government officials and their emails*—from Damian Reese, at the Carl T. Hayden Veterans Administration Medical Center in Phoenix, in which he wrote, "I think it's unfair to call any of this a success when veterans are waiting six weeks on an electronic waiting list *before* they're called to schedule their first PCP [primary-care provider] appointment."

Veterans have to wait six weeks to see a doctor!

Unbelievable!

In Mexico, American veterans can a doctor the next day. In Canada, it's no more than a week.

Then, in September 2013, Mitchell filed a confidential complaint intended for the VA Office of Inspector General, channeled through Senator John McCain's office.

What does McCain, War Hero, do?

He sent her complaint to the Office of Congressional and Legislative Affairs and eventually back to the Veterans

74

Administration. Mitchell, as a result of McCain snitching on her, was placed on administrative leave, part of retaliation.

Retaliation because McCain snitched on her like a fucking traitor!

Can you believe it? Can you believe that an *American* stepping up to *defend* our veterans is *punished* by the Veterans Administration?

And can you believe that "War Hero" John McCain was the asshole who, instead of congratulating her for stepping forward, goes around and, to protect Obama's mismanagement of the Veterans Administration, snitches on her!

Maybe John McCain deserves to be locked up in a cave again!

Obama called the situation "intolerable" and "disgraceful."

Then he went to play golf.

The following month, Dr. Sam Foote, a doctor of internal medicine at the Phoenix Veterans Administration, filed a complaint with the Veterans Administration Office of Inspector General alleging that the so-called "successes" in reducing wait times stem from manipulation of data, and that vets were *dying* while awaiting appointments for medical care. By the end of year, Dr. Foote retired—and became a whistle-blower when he met with *Arizona Republic* reporter Dennis Wagner. Dr. Foote detailed allegations that patients had died while awaiting care at the Phoenix Veterans Administration and that wait time records had been falsified.

Obama called the situation "intolerable" and "disgraceful."

Then he went to play golf.

Then, in January 2014, CNN reported that 19 veterans had died at Veterans Administration hospitals in 2010 and 2011 because of delays in diagnosis and treatment.

President Obama called the situation "intolerable" and "disgraceful."

Then he went to play golf.

In April, it's revealed that at least 40 veterans died while waiting for appointments to see their doctors at the Phoenix Veterans Affairs Healthcare.

In May, Veterans groups called for Secretary of Veterans Affairs Eric Shinseki to resign. White House spokesman Jay Carney told the press that President Obama "remains confident in Secretary Shinseki's ability to lead the department and take appropriate action."

Days later, the House Veterans Affairs Committee voted to subpoena Shinseki and other officials in connection to the Phoenix scandal.

Then it was revealed that the same thing was being done in Wyoming, this "gaming the system." The week after that, Loser Shinseki testified before the Senate Veterans Affairs Committee. "Any allegation, any adverse incident like this makes me mad as hell," Loser Shinseki said, trying to defend the indefensible.

Do you believe him? Do you believe him?

I sure as hell don't! And I don't think you believe him either!

So now they admit they were cooking the books and falsifying data on how the veterans were being treated. And the next week, three supervisors at the Gainesville, Florida, Veterans Administration hospital were placed on paid leave after investigators found a list of patients requiring follow-up care kept on paper, not in their computerized scheduling system.

Then the Office of the Inspector General announced it was investigating 26 agency facilities for allegations of doctored waiting times.

President Obama called the situation "intolerable" and "disgraceful."

He then went to a basketball game to shoot selfies with Beyoncé.

Now, I love Beyoncé! I think she's a Ten. I'm sure you agree Beyoncé's a Ten.

Did you hear that, Heidi Klum? A woman can do anything she wants to do! A woman can have *kids* and still be a Ten!

Did you hear *that*, Heidi Klum?

By the end of the month, a preliminary report from the Veteran Administration's Inspector General's office revealed systemic problems at health facilities nationwide, and that there were serious, serious, serious management and scheduling issues in Phoenix.

At the end of May, Obama accepted Eric Shinseki's resignation.

Is this what it has come down to? Is this how veterans are treated by this administration?

When I'm President Trump, there will be a complete overhaul of the Veterans Administration.

And while it is being overhauled, because, quite frankly, it takes time to do things right if you want to do things right, that doesn't mean our vets will be ignored.

Veterans will be able to go to private hospitals, public hospitals—*anywhere and everywhere*—and the government will reimburse those hospitals for the bills.

Any veterans will be able get the treatment they need.

They won't have to wait for weeks to see a Veterans Administration doctor. They won't have to go to Mexico. They won't have to depend on Wounded Warriors for charity.

When we debated at the Ronald Reagan Presidential Library— Reagan liked me and I liked him and we got along well—I wrote to CNN, asking them to donate the money from that debate to the veterans.

Quite frankly, even with modesty, you have to admit that the ratings for that debate went through the roof because of me!

Trust me, no one was dying to hear what Low-Energy Loser Jeb had to say about anything!

They tuned into CNN to see me!

And I wrote a letter to Jeff Zucker, and it said, "I had always felt that we have to be helping our veterans far more than we do. That is why my campaign is so focused on these great people who have done so much for us. This large contribution of many millions of dollars would be a truly wonderful thing for CNN to do."

He didn't do it.

He kept millions and millions of dollars that they got in ratings because I was in the debate that CNN would not have gotten otherwise.

That kind of greed stops. It has to stop!

We're going to make our military so big and so strong and so great. It will be so powerful that I don't think we're ever going to have to use it. Nobody's going to mess with us.

We have illegal immigrants treated better at our hospitals than our veterans.

I want our veterans to come back from Mexico and Canada and live in the country for which they fought!

I thank Mexico and I thank Canada but, under a Trump administration, we won't be forcing our vets to leave America to get the health care they need!

I want our vets to get the best medical care in the world here at home!

Make America Great Again!

Vote Trump.

8. We Must End the Tyranny of Political Correctness

Our leaders are stupid!

We have—for two generations now—been bamboozled and shamed into political correctness.

Political correctness stifles free speech.

I think the big problem this country has is being politically correct. I've been challenged by so many people and I don't, frankly, have time for total political correctness. And to be honest with you, this country doesn't have time, either.

And, in fact, I want to challenge the entire notion of political correctness.

Did you know?

Did you know that political correctness is a weapon used by the Democrats and the Left to oppress minorities?

It's true!

Political correctness is a weapon Democrats use to suppress women!

Political correctness is a linguistic form of modern-day slavery that strives to keep blacks, Hispanics, and Asians shackled to second-class status!

Political correctness is a weapon Democrats use to attack Latinos!

Advocates of political correctness want to control your thoughts, your speech, and your beliefs.

These are serious haters.

And these haters are disguised as your friends.

It's very simple to see.

Look at the *New York Times*!

The! New! York! Times!

That bastion of liberalism—and liberal bigotry!

The! New! York! Times!

Let me remind you how—under the guise of political correctness—the *New York Times* mocks, disparages, ridicules, and belittles Latinos!

It's true!

The Pope!

When Pope Francis was in New York, he went to a school in Harlem. At that school, parents were invited to meet the pope.

It turns out that Juan Tapia and his wife, Agueda Zavaleta, were invited to meet the pope. Juan Tapia and Agueda Zavaleta are immigrants from Mexico. They are indigenous people from Oaxaca who, by the way, don't even speak Spanish fluently, since they speak an indigenous—or Native American—language.

So, anyway, these illegal aliens—let me be clear that there's no way in the world the American Embassy in the Mexico City gave immigration visas to Oaxacan peasants to come to the United States—were on their way to meet Pope Francis.

Good for them.

I'd like to meet the pope.

Wouldn't you?

You don't have to be Catholic and pray to wax figures to want to have a great selfie with Pope Francis!

So the *New York Times*, ever the bastion of liberalism and proponent of political correctness, sends a reporter to interview these illegal aliens on their way to meet the pope.

I have the article right here. This is how the *New York Times* begins the story: "This week brought Pope Francis to the South Lawn of the White House, where he spoke to a crowd of thousands and greeted President Obama. It brought Juan Tapia to a house outside Yonkers, where he spent days painting the living room blue — 'the color of the sky today,' he said on Thursday."

Who wrote this?

Vivian Yee.

Yee?

80

Obviously the Chinese Exclusion Act of 1882 didn't do its job, did it?

So Vivian Yee, this Chinese-American reporter for the *New York Times*, described how Juan and Agueda prepared to go on a trip of lifetime: Oaxacan peasants, illegal aliens in New York, going to the school where their anchor baby, also known as their U.S.–born daughter, goes to school.

Vivian Yee—"Yee" is a Cantonese Chinese name, did you know that?

Vivian Yee, a smug, politically correct bigot, then mocks the illegals. She writes: "In modest finery and gaudy costumes, the group stood out on the train."

Let me tell you something.

What she calls "gaudy costumes," Diana Vreeland called "fabulous."

What she calls "gaudy costumes" was all the rage when Frida Kahlo—and her millions of fans around the world—loved to wear them.

Let me tell you something.

Have you heard of Pineda Covalín?

If you haven't, then your wife isn't spending thousands and thousands of dollars buying up the expensive, expensive, expensive articles of accessories that this Mexican designer sells.

Believe me!

Scarves! Clutches! Accessories!

They have a shop here in SoHo—and these fashions, mocked as "gaudy" by Vivian Yee when worn by Latino peasants—are all the rage when worn by Anglos.

The bigotry!

Is it politically correct to make fun of peasants living in our country who don't speak English? Would Pope Francis mock their "gaudy costumes"?

And by the way, who is Vivian Yee to bitch about their "modest finery," anyway? I'm sure *her* finery is modest compared to anything my wife has!

I'm sure this racist Asian reporter doesn't have an account at Harry Winston, that's for sure!

But it gets worse.

She writes, "When the pope walked in, Mr. Tapia wanted to cry. At the appointed moment, as Mr. Tapia watched, Ms. Zavaleta stepped forward with her altar linens, in her red-green-and-white dress, to greet the man they had seen only on television."

The. Man. They. Had. Seen. Only. On. Television.

And Vivian Yee sees the pope every day? I'll bet *this* was the *first* time she *saw* the pope in person—whom she had only seen on television *before* he came to New York!

Give *me* a break! Give *America* a break!

The point I want to make in reading Vivian Yee's condescending report, "A Day Laborer, on His Way to See Pope Francis," is that American liberals *mock* Latinos all the time—and they use political correctness as a cover for their bigotry.

Vivian Yee and the *New York Times* are making fun of the Oaxacan nation!

That article, in my opinion, constitutes hate speech directed against the indigenous people of Oaxaca—who, by the way, are illegals in the U.S., and I will deport them back to their homelands.

Why?

Quite, frankly, there's no need for a Oaxacan Diaspora in New York, thank you very much.

Why?

Because they don't assimilate—learn English, become Americans. They are walking around clueless about what it means to be Americans—or even New Yorkers!

We want people who live here to be in a New York state of mind, not a Oaxacan state of mindlessness!

Let's face it! These illegals fled Oaxaca and, like most illegals, they are *economic* refugees living in the shadows of American society.

This is terrible, terrible, terrible!

And this situation is encouraged by proponents of political correctness who want peasants coming to America to remain peasants living in America.

That's what's happening.

So, in the final analysis, political correctness, an intellectual scam feigning interest in human interest stories and human interest concerns, disguises prejudice.

Were Juan and Agueda concerned about how they were ridiculed by this racist Asian reporter?

I don't think they give a fuck about the *New York Times*. They met Pope Francis, a dream come true, and the bigots at the *New York Times* can go fuck themselves.

Trust me, I've met reporters from the *New York Times* — and they dress like they shop at outlet malls and buy junk jewelry at JCPenney.

But in this campaign nobody — EXCEPT ME — is defending these Mexican peasants, letting Vivian Yee's "politically correct" bigotry slide.

Where is Jorge Ramos?

Jorge Ramos, the man who pontificated out of turn at my news conference in Iowa and won't sit down and wait his turn, is nowhere to be seen defending his fellow wetbacks.

I didn't see him stand up to Vivian Yee's racist mocking of these Oaxacan peasant illegals in New York. I didn't see him condemn Vivian Yee's editors at the *New York Times* — who, by the way, are guilty of letting this bigotry get published.

I'm not surprised.

I'm not surprised as one set of Leftist Losers at Univision covers up for another set of Leftist Losers at the *New York Times*, are you?

Did you know that Jorge Ramos came to the U.S. on a student visa? Did you know he then got a job in L.A.?

Hello? A *student* visa is not a *work* visa!

Thank you for breaking our laws, you loser beaner.

And on top of everything, Jorge Ramos's daughter works for

Hillary Clinton—but he'd never disclose that, would he?

Give *me* a break! Give *America* a break!

Vivian Yee is just one example of how Democrats and Liberals use political correctness to attack Latinos—and other minorities.

Want a more important example?

Nancy Pelosi.

Yes, Nancy Pelosi, that racist piece of human shit.

She's from San Francisco. She represents California's 12th Congressional District, which includes most of San Francisco.

But you wouldn't know it when you consider her complete indifference to how political correctness is used as a weapon in San Francisco to attack Latinos!

I've spoken at length about beautiful, beautiful, beautiful Kate Steinle who was killed in San Francisco by that Mexican killer and illegal, Francisco López Sánchez.

It's a tragedy! It's a tragedy!

Her death is the reason we must secure our border.

But I want to talk about *another* Hispanic from San Francisco.

Ever hear of Edgar Mora?

Edgar Mora, who is legal, by the way, was savagely attacked by advocates of political correctness" who have brought ruin to San Francisco's Latino residents.

Edgar Mora was falsely prosecuted for a hate crime he did not commit by San Francisco District Attorney Terence Hallinan.

Terence Hallinan, a racist piece of human shit, was running for reelection. He needed the votes of "politically correct" bigots in San Francisco.

Since political correctness dictates that Latinos be vilified by the Looney Loser Left—did you see how they desecrated the religious mission where Saint Junípero Serra is buried a week after he was canonized?—Hallinan falsely charged Edgar Mora with a hate crime.

Just. To. Win. Reelection.

Where was Nancy Pelosi when a Mexican human rights organization appealed to her office to defend Latinos and take a stand against Terence Hallinan, that racist piece of human shit?

Democratic racist pieces of human shit stick together.

That's why Hillary Hippo Hips Hypocrite is counting on winning California!

Nancy Pelosi, that racist piece of human shit, is also from San Francisco, and is also a Hillary Hippo Hips Hypocrite cheerleader!

And it gets worse!

Dianne Feinstein, who's so stupid she needs a double assassination to advance her political career, is also from San Francisco—and covering up San Francisco city government's anti-Latino bigotry!

Terence Hallinan, who is both a racist piece of human shit and an opportunistic media whore, used political correctness in San Francisco to attack Edgar Mora, a Latino.

Where was Jorge Ramos when this was happening?

Was he a student? Was he working illegally?

Was he honing his skills as an activist pretending to be a journalist?

He wasn't there, challenging Nancy Pelosi—who, by the way, is an enemy of legal Hispanics as her record in Congress shows—who did nothing, nothing, nothing while Terence Hallinan destroyed an innocent man's life—just so he could win reelection.

Political correctness is a disease the Left has spread throughout our society.

In the case of Edgar Mora, did you know that San Francisco taxpayers were funding an organization that *coached* the prosecution witness to testify *falsely* against Mr. Mora?

Telling a witness what to say is witness tampering! It's obstruction of justice!

But if it is done by Liberals attacking Latinos, then it's okay.

Why?

I guess it's because it's "politically correct" hatred!

In the same way Vivian Yee—whose grandmother, I'll bet, walked around in a gaudy costume balancing a basket of dog meat on her head on her way to some smelly open-air Cantonese market in nowhere China—gets away with mocking two Mexican peasant illegals, racists in San Francisco get away with attacking Latinos.

The prosecution witness against Mr. Mora was Timothy Carroll, a drug addict. Timothy Carroll, this wreckage of a human being, was then contacted by Lester Olmstead-Rose, a racist piece of human shit, and was told what to say on the witness stand.

Lester Olmstead-Rose was the director of some loser organization—which, by the way, I consider to be an anti-Latino hate group—that got funds from the city. And this organization got drug addict Timothy Carroll to change his testimony.

What did Nancy Pelosi, that racist piece of human shit, do?

Nothing.

In San Francisco, it's politically correct to attack Latinos.

The jury didn't buy Terence Hallinan's malicious prosecution of an innocent Latino, thank goodness.

Is that old racist fuck still alive?

But the point is that despicable racists like Lester Olmstead-Rose—who, by the way, lost his job over his brazen witness tampering and obstruction of justice—used political correctness to attack Latinos.

Now, that racist fuck works for La Piana Consulting, so you can just imagine what kind of fucked-up place that is if it hires anti-Latino bigots who coached drug addict Timothy Carroll to testify falsely against Edgar Mora just so Lester Olmstead-Rose could advance his own political ambitions in that anti-Latino city of San Francisco!

And all these politically correct fascists are going to be out on the streets when I'm done!

Nobody in this race is talking about this—except me!

Nobody is talking about the fascism of political correctness— except me!

Nobody is talking about how important it is to speak the truth in America!

86

Fat pig Rosie O'Donnell is not "calorically challenged." She's a fat pig.

Sanguine Megyn Kelly is not "intellectually deprived." She's a bimbo.

Hillary Hippo Hips Hypocrite is not "sartorially impaired." She dresses like a giant, fat, blue robin!

Huma, wife of Sleazebag Jew, is not "religiously observant." She's an oppressed Muslim female who has no self-respect and stays married to a sick fuck Perv!

Hey, Huma, ever hear of Helen Reddy?

She's the Australian feminist who sings "I Am Woman! Hear Me Roar!"

Well, you can roar, too!

Be empowered and walk away from that mess of a sleazebag!

You can't remain a stupid, submissive Muslim piece of human shit for the rest of your life!

Who wants to be like Nancy Pelosi, that racist piece of human shit who did nothing, nothing, nothing while Edgar Mora was falsely prosecuted!

She's a sleazebag, that Nancy Pelosi—in addition to being a racist piece of human shit.

But sleazebags are what Hillary Hippo Hips Hypocrite surrounds herself with.

Take Gavin Newsom.

He was mayor of—where else?—San Francisco—Ground Zero for politically correct attacks on Latinos.

Do I need to remind you about Gavin Newsom? He's another sleazebag.

So here's the story on this asshole, the former mayor of San Francisco who wants to be the governor of California.

Now Gavin Newsom, he's the mayor of San Francisco, right? And because being mayor of that city means there's nothing to do—since politically correct attacks on Latinos are on autopilot—he has all this free time on his hands. And a young guy with all the free time in the world on his hands has to do something with his hands.

Why not feel up a beautiful woman?

In January 2007, it was revealed that Gavin Newsom had been having a romantic relationship Ruby Rippey-Tourk.

Who is Ruby Rippey-Tourk?

She's a beautiful woman. She's also the wife of his former deputy chief of staff and then campaign manager, Alex Tourk!

Not only does this sleazebag commit adultery by sleeping with his best friend's wife, but his best friend is also his campaign manager.

What! A! Sleazebag!

You'd think that a despicable sleazebag's political career would be over.

But guess what?

He was voted Lieutenant Governor! And now he's running for Governor!

Give *me* a break! Give *America* a break!

And it gets better—or worse, depending on your viewpoint, whether you are for or against *Scum in Government.*

Gavin Newsom supports Hillary Clinton for President!

Why not?

Bill Clinton did the same thing: commit adultery in the Oval Office by taking advantage of a young woman, Monica Lewinsky.

This is how Hillary Hippo Hips Hypocrite wants to be elected president!

Hillary Hippo Hips Hypocrite is trying to galvanize the Sleazebag-American vote in order to win. She has to—that is, of course, if she's the nominee, which I doubt because of her email scandal. But if she survives the nomination/coronation process, she wants every Sleazebag in America to vote for her.

Well, not me.

I don't want the Sleazebag-American vote.

I want the Decent-American vote!

I want decent, law-abiding, God-fearing Americans to vote for me!

Decent, hardworking Americans who love their country and want the U.S. to be great again—those are my supporters!

But not Hillary Hippo Hips Hypocrite!

She wants sleazebags to support her when she and her sleazebag husband return to the Oval Office.

She wants the support of the Great Sleazebag of the East, Anthony Weiner, and the support of the Great Sleazebag of the West, Gavin Newsom!

And no one says anything because being a Sleazebag for Hillary is politically correct!

Can you imagine if Hillary Hippo Hips Hypocrite wins?

Can you imagine a day when the Three Sleazebags are in the Oval Office together?

Bill Clinton. Anthony Weiner. Gavin Newsom?

Give *me* a break! Give *America* a break!

Where is Crybaby Jorgito Güerito Ramosito?

¿El pendejito estúpido?

Not in sight!

So, if Jorge Ramos and Univision are *not* prepared to stand up for Latinos, then I am!

I say NO to "politically correct" attacks on Latinos!

But instead of joining me, Jorge Ramos—can you believe this fucking wetback?—has the nerve to say, "Right now Donald Trump is, no question, the loudest voice of intolerance, hatred, and division in the United States."

What?

I'm not the one engaging in witness tampering and obstruction of justice by telling a drug addict prosecution witness how to bear false witness against an innocent Latino!

I'm not the anti-Latino bigot betting I can get reelected by maliciously prosecuting a Latino!

Where is Jorge Ramos's outrage at that despicable anti-Latino bigot Lester Olmstead-Rose?

Where is Jorge Ramos's outrage at that putrid anti-Latino bigot Terence Hallinan?

Where are the Univision's news trucks hounding Nancy Pelosi, that racist piece of human shit, or Gavin Newsom, another racist piece of human shit?

That shithead attacks me when I'm the only one standing up and speaking for the Silent Hispanic Majority!

I say NO to using political correctness to attack Latinos and other minorities!

I say NO to liberal hypocrites who are now using political correctness to control our thoughts, our speech, and our right to speak the truth!

Political correctness is a fascist instrument that uses speech to repress the weakest among us.

Will I deport Juan Tapia and Agueda Zavaleta?

They sound like wonderful people, but if they broke the law and are here as illegals, then, yes, they have to go back.

They have to go back to the beautiful hills and valleys of Oaxaca.

But, at the same time, will I defend Edgar Mora, a legal Hispanic in this country?

You better believe that I will defend Mr. Mora against the likes of Terence Hallinan, a racist piece of human shit; Lester Olmstead-Rose, another piece of human shit; and, of course, Nancy Pelosi, the biggest piece of human shit that has ever come to Congress from San Francisco.

And that's saying a lot because, as we all know, Dianne Feinstein is another monumental piece of human shit that has come out of the rectum of San Francisco!

When I'm president, the tyranny of political correctness ends!

Make America Great Again!

Vote Trump.

9. America Must Be a Nation of Winners, Not Victims!

Our leaders are stupid!

America, the idea of America and the reality of America, is what we hold dear!

America is a global brand!

It's true.

To billions and billions of people around the world, when they think of America they think of the American Dream, because this is the land of opportunity.

But is America living up to its reputation, that we are a nation of winners?

I don't think so. I don't think so.

I don't think that Americans see themselves as winners any longer.

Can you blame us?

Look at the stupid, stupid, stupid leaders we have! Look at how incompetent, so completely incompetent they are.

Congress can't get anything done—and when it does, it's a disaster that makes things worse. The Supreme Court thinks it can "reinterpret" the Constitution to legislate from the bench. And as for the president—we all know the losers, losers, losers that we have had!

And have now!

Bush I, who negotiated that NAFTA trade deal that has destroyed millions and millions of good-paying American jobs.

Clinton, who made more bad trade deals, did nothing when Al Qaeda first attacked the U.S.—remember the FIRST attack on the World Trade Center? Remember the bombings of two of our embassies in Africa? Remember the attack on the USS *Cole?*

That was Osama bin Laden!

And Clinton didn't get him when he had the chance to get him.

Then, Bush II, who was—*and is*—so stupid he went into Iraq, a war that was a disaster, a complete disaster, the worst disaster in our nation's history.

And now, Obama, a terrible, terrible, terrible president who is more interested in shooting selfies with Beyoncé than in running the country.

I admit, Beyoncé is a Ten, but come on, if you're president you have work to do!

And it is because we have had such weak, ineffectual—and, by the way, loser—presidents that Americans no longer see themselves as winners.

That's my perception. And, believe me, my perception is very, very, very good.

It has to be!

I didn't make billions and billions of dollars by not being perceptive!

And my perceptions are backed up by research. The Pew Research Center confirms what I *perceive* to be true.

I have it right here!

And I quote: "As they look to their own future and that of their children, many in the lower class see their prospects dimming. About three-quarters (77%) say it's harder now to get ahead than it was ten years ago. Only half (51%) say that hard work brings success, a view expressed by overwhelming majorities of those in the middle (67%) and upper classes (71%). While the expectation that each new generation will surpass their parents is a central tenet of the American Dream, those lower classes are significantly more likely than middle- or upper-class adults to believe their children will have a worse standard of living than they do."

Let me repeat this: "Americans believe their children will have a worse standard of living than they do."

This thinking makes me sick! It's un-American!

It's un-American to think that tomorrow will be worse that

today!

What would Ronald Reagan say if he knew that Americans today believe tomorrow will be worse than today?

The only people who believe this are losers!

That Americans now believe this to be true is an *abomination!*

That's not who we are! Americans are not losers!

But because we have such stupid, stupid, stupid leaders, that's the sad state of our nation today.

Is American the land of *disappointment?* Is it the land of *diminished expectations?* Is it the land where the standards of living will *continue to decline?*

It can't be true!

But we have leaders who continue to disappoint us.

Do you know how disgusted I was when Bill Clinton forced himself on that young intern? What a disgusting Perv. Do you know how disappointed I was when Bush II launched that failed war of invasion against Iraq? It's cost us $2.5 trillion dollars, and we got nothing but ISIS to show for it. Do you know how disappointed I am in Obama's lack of achievements? I am still incredulous that we have a do-nothing president who just wants to shoot selfies with celebrities and play golf!

And if you think I'm being mean, that's what the WORLD thinks of Obama!

A.

Big.

Black.

Disappointment.

That Kenyan Socialist is a big, black disappointment to Americans—and to the world!

How many of you know who Geir Lundestad is?

A show of hands!

Not many.

I thought so!

Geir Lundestad is the former secretary of the Nobel Peace Prize committee. He just published a memoir in which he discusses the 2009 award of the Nobel Peace Prize to Barack Obama.

Now, Geir Lundestad worked at the Nobel Institute for 25 years, so he has been around for a long time. He knows the ins and outs of that institution.

Do you know what he wrote in his memoir?

I have it right here!

Geir Lundestad wrote: "In hindsight, we could say that the argument of giving Obama a helping hand was only partially correct."

What a lovely, diplomatic way of saying that Obama did not meet the expectations the Nobel Prize committee had for him—because Obama is a LOSER!

Geir Lundestad writes that the decision to give Obama the award was unanimous, but that it was intended to help him achieve his ambitious goals. And the truth is that the U.S. president's record since receiving the prize showed it was a mistake to have given him the Nobel Peace Prize.

A terrible, terrible, terrible mistake.

He didn't *deserve* the Nobel Peace Prize, and now the Nobel Institute acknowledges it made a *mistake* in giving it to him!

If they could, they'd take the Nobel Peace Prize back!

The world wants to believe Americans are winners, and we are confronted with the reality that we are—now—a nation of losers.

And this state of being LOSERS is overtaking our entire society.

I live in New York.

I'm proud of New York. But I'm also realistic and honest.

Is New York the greatest city in the world?

It can be, but it isn't.

New York isn't the greatest city in the world when we have a Third-World airport like LaGuardia. What a disaster!

New York isn't the greatest city in the world when we have Third-World potholes all over the place—and our infrastructure is falling apart everywhere.

New York isn't the greatest city in the world when we need to have a lunch program in the summer because so many children in New York live in such poverty that if the city didn't feed them *one hot meal a day* during school recess, these kids wouldn't have *any* nutritious meals at all during the summer.

New York isn't the greatest city in the world as long as a third of all New Yorkers are on some form of public assistance.

And, to my way of thinking, New Yorkers have come to think of themselves as LOSERS and VICTIMS since September 11.

Did you know that?

Did you know that there is an active movement for New Yorkers to think of themselves as losers and victims?

And that this is a direct consequence of September 11?

Why?

Let me tell you why.

It is because we have conditioned Americans into believing that government will solve *all* their problems and give them all the money they need *as long as they are victims.*

Did you know that?

Did you know that if you go to the government and whine and whine and whine, just to shut you up, they'll give you money to go away and stop whining?

Give *me* a break! Give *America* a break!

That's what's happened because of the stupid, stupid, stupid leaders we elect!

Take Ground Zero.

It was terrible, what happened there, the destruction of the World Trade Center and the deaths of thousands of innocents.

But there's a difference between being a *victim* and being a *hero.*

We now have this narrative — *this myth* — that all the people who died on September 11 are heroes.

True, many were, particularly the firefighters, police, and emergency first responders who rushed in to help and were killed. *Those* are *heroes.*

But many of the civilians killed did nothing heroic: *They were victims.*

Let me give you an example.

Do you think Christine Hanson is a hero? Do you think she did anything heroic?

I'll bet you don't know who Christine Hanson was.

Christine Hanson was a passenger on American Airlines Flight 11. She was three years old. Her parents, Peter and Susan Hanson, were taking her to Disneyland in California.

The three of them died when their hijacked airplane slammed into the North Tower.

It's a tragedy!

It's a horror!

It's a horrible, horrible, horrible tragedy!

But that doesn't make Christine Hanson a hero in any understanding of what the word *hero* means.

She's a victim.

But by enshrining everyone who died as a hero—again, many were, but not all—we cheapen the integrity of language.

At Ground Zero what we really have, if you want to know the truth, is a celebration of grief.

Under the direction of Alice Greenwald—who, by the way, is the former director of the Holocaust Museum, so you know she's in the business of putting on horror shows—Ground Zero has become a moneymaking Grief Fest.

If Americans, as the Pew Research Center confirms, now see themselves as losers, the reason for this is that we are surrounded by stupid, stupid, stupid people in positions of authority.

Alice Greenwald exploits the memory of those who died on September 11 to create a macabre spectacle that makes money.

That's what it is: Ground Zero is a circus show of grief that exploits both *heroes*—like the firefighters and police—and *victims*—like Christine Hanson—to make money, money, money.

Did you know that?

Did you know that the National September 11 Memorial & Museum is being marketed as a celebration of death and destruction? I'll show you how it's being done.

Every year, on September 10th, the day before the anniversary, an organization called Voices of September 11 has a meeting. It was dreamed up by Mary Fetchet, and this organization, pretending to be an advocacy group for victims—that's what they call themselves, *victims*, not *heroes*—strategizes on how to get more *money* for the *victims*—not *heroes*—of September 11.

So, do you know what goes on when this group meets?

Of course they strategize on how to shake down more money from Congress, but there's more going on at this horror show of Loser Victims.

Alice Greenwald shows up and talks. Jan Ramírez, who is the Curator for the Museum, also shows up.

And lots of other losers join in this Mourn Fest.

So the first order of business is to recruit new victims.

Can you believe it? Can you believe it?

Mary Fetchet is out there with her "Help Us Enroll One More!" campaign.

One more *what?*

One more *victim!*

Yes, you, too, can be a victim. If on September 11, 2001, you were alive and had a pulse, you qualify to be registered as an official victim!

Can you believe it! Can you believe it!

On September 10, 2015, one day before the 14th anniversary, Mary Fetchet was out there looking for more victims to sign up!

Why?

Because we are a nation of LOSERS!

And it gets worse.

There they were, one day before the 14th anniversary, at the Marriott Hotel, where they have their daylong gathering of September 11 Losers and people still are "processing" their "grief."

Do you know how grief is processed?

Wait until I tell you!

Wait until you hear, America!

They have tables set up with arts and crafts supplies, the kind you find in kindergarten. You know, paints, glue, glitter, and magic markers. And they have official September 11 aprons.

APRONS!

And these assembled losers are invited to make their own arts and crafts September 11 apron—a way to work out their grief, one day shy of the 14th anniversary of the terror attacks!

Can you believe it? Can you believe it?

Give *me* a break! Give *America* a break!

But there they are—like mental retards—decorating September 11 aprons to cope with their grief.

Good grief!

And, it gets better—or worse.

After Mary Fetchet, moron that she is, was done walking around signing up as many more new "victims" as possible, there was an entire day of presentations.

It culminated with Alice Greenwald, the High Priestess in the Cult of Death for the residents of the City of Perpetual Mourning, speaking to the victims assembled.

Of course, all the political scheming on how to get more money from Congress was out of the way, so the crowd was ready to hear from Alice herself.

So, now, I ask you: What did the High Priestess in the Cult of Death for the residents of the City of Perpetual Mourning say?

Are you ready?

Are you ready for the absurdity of it all?

Alice Greenwald opened her mouth and announced that the Museum has increased its ranking on TripAdvisor!

TripAdvisor!

TripAdvisor!

Who gives a fuck about TripAdvisor?

98

Well, Alice Greenwald, High Priestess in the Cult of Death for the residents of the City of Perpetual Mourning, gave a big fuck about it.

In fact, that Loser Bitch won't shut up about TripAdvisor.

And Alice Greenwald then announced that the Museum now ranks up there with the Taj Mahal and Machu Picchu in terms of popularity!

Popularity?

Is that what Ground Zero has become?

A global popularity contest on TripAdvisor?

Disgusting! Despicable!

This bitch is a sick fuck!

This is what she was concerned about: Ground Zero's ranking on TripAdvisor!

You know that crazed bitch Alice Greenwald wakes up each morning and checks Ground Zero's ranking on TripAdvisor.

Loser! Loser! Loser!

But it didn't stop there!

In a city of victims where Americans are all LOSERS, how can it stop there?

Alice Greenwald, High Priestess in the Cult of Death for the residents of the City of Perpetual Mourning, then went on to recap her year—everything wonderful that happened to her since she last addressed the assembled losers.

"I met," she said, "Bon Jovi!"

Gasps of delight from the audience!

BON JOVI!

Give *me* a break! Give *America* a break!

Then she went on, about the TripAdvisor reviews and all the other wonderful people she's met. Alice Greenwald, who exploits the memory of those killed on September 11, then told the audience of morons, all showing off their brand-new arts and crafts September 11 aprons, that Catherine, Duchess of Cambridge, is more beautiful in person than in her pictures.

More gasps from the assembled Loser Victims.

And, she said, Prince William is really tall.

Great, maybe he can play basketball very, very, very well.

Who cares?

The morons—listed as Official Victims of September 11—do!

They gasped in approval.

And it went on!

Alice told them that in a few weeks she was going to meet Pope Francis!

Why couldn't someone shove an official September 11 apron in her mouth to shut the crazed bitch up?

It wouldn't have done any good. The circus continued.

How?

Janice Ramírez, Curator of Relics, told the audience that the "collections"—and I use that word very, very, very liberally—had increased.

Here's a fun fact: Of all the people who died at Ground Zero, only one person was from Arizona. His name was Gary Bird.

And Janice Ramírez announced that his widow donated Gary Bird's horse saddle to the museum. It will be included in the rotating exhibitions of the mementos of those who died.

A horse saddle?

Give *me* a break! Give *America* a break!

Jan Ramírez thinks she's a Curator of Relics. She's not. She's a Collector of Garbage!

If I had been at Windows on the World on the morning of September 11, 2001, and died, you know that Janice Ramírez would have harassed and stalked my wife, Melania, until she "donated" my hairbrush to the Museum.

And they'd put it on view: "This is the hairbrush that Donald J. Trump, a hero of September 11, used to brush his hair for the last time before he left, on that fateful morning, for a breakfast meeting at Windows on the World in the North Tower. Where! He! Perished!"

Of all the trash Janice Ramírez, the Collector of Garbage

masquerading as Curator of Relics, assembled, the one artifact she couldn't curate into that Temple to the Cult of Death is decency!

Crazed bitch Alice Greenwald has transformed Ground Zero into the global epicenter of the Cult of Death!

Gary Bird and his horse saddle!

Ridiculous!

Send that horse saddle back to the Gary Bird's widow explaining that the National September 11 Memorial and Museum is not Goodwill Industries!

Give *me* a break! Give *America* a break!

Janice Ramírez is one creepy, sick fuck! What this Collector of Garbage has done is something out of the Medieval Ages—memento mori!

In a cemetery!

And that's what that museum is: A cemetery.

Why?

Because there are human remains there! It's not a museum; it's an underground *mausoleum* at Ground Zero!

These unidentified human remains, which are venerated as if they were Jesus Christ's foreskin—the only part of his body left on earth—could very well include remains of the hijackers!

What?

Yes!

That's sick!

And just as sick is the commercial exploitation of our September 11 dead!

This is something only depraved people do!

This is disgusting! This is despicable!

And this disgusting, despicable Alice Greenwald was more interested in TripAdvisor than anything else!

What is one to make of this stupid, stupid, stupid crazed bitch at Ground Zero?

No wonder Americans believe tomorrow will be worse than today!

In America, there are no Sacred Cows!

If you want to *milk* a Sacred *Cash* Cow, you disgusting, despicable Alice Greenwald, then go to India, but get the fuck out of New York!

New Yorkers are not losers! New Yorkers are not victims!

New Yorkers are Americans!

And Americans are WINNERS!

But you wouldn't know it!

The Pew Research Center reports most Americans believe their children will be worse off because we are no longer a nation of winners.

Is that surprising?

It's not!

When you have a LOSER president more interested in selfies with Beyoncé than in fighting ISIS, what else can you expect?

When you have a moron like Mary Fetchet, like the LOSER that she is, walking around New York looking to sign up more victims of September 11 —*fourteen years after the terror attacks*—what else can you expect?

When you have a LOSER like Janice Ramírez stalking the families of dead for toothbrushes, combs, shoes, and —*yes*—horse saddles, what else can you expect?

When you have a LOSER like crazed bitch Alice Greenwald looking forward to meeting rock stars, what else can you expect?

These people are fucks so sick they are sick fucks!

The United States is not some medieval nation with dried-up bones and toothbrushes on display in Temples of Death masquerading as museums!

This is not who we are as a people!

But there they are, the three harpies: Alice Greenwald, Janice Ramírez, and Mary Fetchet, smug and self-congratulating narcissists, who think that their pathetic Cult of Death is what America wants!

Leave the celebrations of the dead to the Mexicans and their Day of the Dead bullshit! New York is not Oaxaca!

102

New York is America!

And America is about life!

America is about the future!

America is not about displaying the toothbrushes and horse saddles of people who suffered tragic deaths at the hands of terrorists for a voyeuristic public that hungers for a macabre spectacle that only a deranged Holocaust horror-show impresario could invent!

This is not the America we want!

Americans are not weak!

We are not cowards! We don't bow down to the Cult of Death!

We do not sign up to be listed as official victims by the government forevermore!

WE ARE NOT LOSERS!

When I'm in the White House, Americans will be winners again!

Make America Great Again!

Vote Trump.

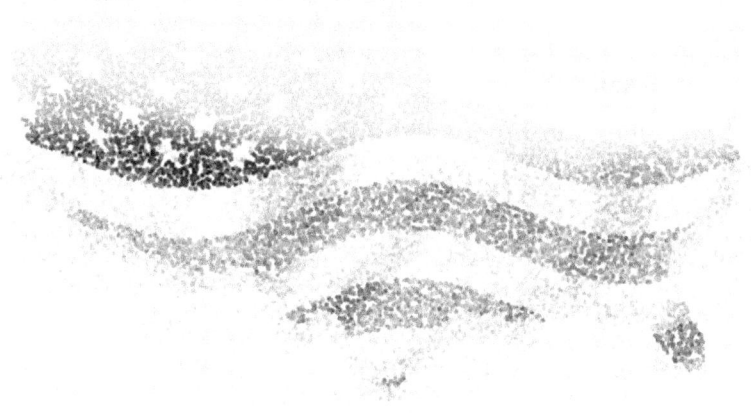

10. We Must Restore the American Dream

Our leaders are stupid!

Our leaders believe they can destroy the American Dream and still have a great country.

That's wrong!

We are only a great country if our people have hope.

And the American Dream is the greatest hope humankind ever created!

The American Dream is dead—but I'm going to restore it, and it's going to be bigger and better and stronger than ever before!

The American Dream! It's going to be better than ever before!

I promise you that!

The Democrats deceive, pretending to lead.

They don't lead. They follow.

They follow cultural changes and they follow Supreme Court decisions—and they appropriate both as their own!

This has destroyed the American Dream, where our students leave college with crushing debt, where our seniors have to decide whether to buy food or their prescriptions, where the middle class is an endangered species.

I've made a fortune—a fabulous fortune—by knowing how to make the kinds of the decisions that create wealth, fabulous wealth.

That's why—let's face it—I'm fabulously wealthy!

But I'm running for office because the country needs me.

Yes, cynics say that I'm doing it for my brand. And that's bullshit. I already have one of the greatest brands in the world!

I think, quite honestly, that only Coca-Cola is a better brand than Trump.

But as we embark on this journey to restore the American Dream—this long and selfless journey—we must have a moral compass to guide us.

It's not that the American Dream is about materialism—although, to be honest, there's nothing wrong with living well.

But it is more than that.

It is about the future. It is about hope. It is about who we are as a people.

It is what Ronald Reagan envisioned when he gave the commencement address at William Woods College in June 1952. This is what Ronald Reagan, in whose selfless steps of public service I am now following, said: "I, in my own mind, have always thought of America as a place in the divine scheme of things that was set aside as a promised land. It was set here and the price of admission was very simple: The means of selection was very simple as to how this land should be populated. Any place in the world and any person from those places; any person with the courage, with the desire to tear up roots, to strive for freedom, to attempt and dare to live in a strange and foreign place, to travel halfway across the world was welcome here."

He said that. He said that because that—*desire*—is what fuels the American Dream!

Anyone willing to obey our laws, is welcome to come here!

And for us Americans who were born here or have become naturalized citizens, the American Dream must be restored and placed within reach.

I know my strengths and weaknesses.

Believe me I do!

I am terrific at making deals, running businesses, making money, and creating jobs.

That's what I do. That's what I've done all my life. That's what has made me one of the richest men in the world who owns some of the most iconic buildings ever built.

I know I do not have the oratory that others have.

I don't, for instance, have the gift of communication like Ronald Reagan did.

But if we are to be a nation of WINNERS again, we must leave

LOSER politicians behind.

Think of all the people running. Do any of them inspire you? Do any of them have the energy and the vision that Americans want? Do any of them have proven track records of success?

Do any of them remind you of the strength, moral clarity, and vision of Ronald Reagan?

May I remind you of his final address to the nation?

He said, "I've spoken of the shining city all my political life. . . . And how stands the city on this winter night? . . . After 200 years, two centuries, she still stands strong and true to the granite ridge, and her glow has held no matter what storm. And she's still a beacon, still a magnet for all who must have freedom, for all the pilgrims from all the lost places who are hurting through the darkness, toward home."

Would he agree with that today?

Would he look at the shambles that remains of the American Dream and be proud?

Our country has gone terribly wrong, wrong, wrong since September 11, 2001.

We have launched ill-conceived wars of invasion. We have become a nation that tortures. We have built a temple to the Cult of Death at Ground Zero. We have lost the respect of friends—and more importantly, our adversaries around the world no longer fear us.

Our borders have been breached by an army of illegals. Our nation is under constant cyberattack by false friends. Our standing in the world is being challenged by Russia and China.

Americans are abducted by terrorists and they are beheaded on television. Our military has been ordered to protect child rapists. We hold people in clandestine prisons around the world. We operate "black sites" where detainees are subjected to torture.

We live under a constant, fabricated, and false sense of fear. We are brainwashed into thinking there is imminent danger every waking hour. We are subjected to security screenings before we board planes and have SWAT teams patrolling Grand Central Station.

We live like cowards.

And this is wrong.

In the land of the free and the home of the brave, men, women—and intersex persons—are subjected to the constant drone of hysteria.

We must live like the free and the brave.

That's why I'm putting the people on notice who are coming here from Syria as part of this mass migration that if I win—*and I will win*—they are going back. This could be one of the great tactical ploys of all time, a 200,000-man army. We have no way of knowing who these people are, and we have enough of a challenge restoring the American Dream for Americans.

We cannot afford—that's how degraded our country has become under Bush II and Obama—to absorb this many people from that troubled part of the world.

America for Americans and the American Dream must be restored for the American people first and foremost.

If we are going to be deporting illegals, millions of them, we cannot be in a position of giving asylum to troubled people from troubled lands—and incur the risk of undermining our national security.

The American Dream is built on strength, not on incurring reckless risks.

It's that simple.

It's time the American government put the interests of the American people first. It's time we showed generosity to our own people—whose hopes, aspirations, and dreams have been undermined by this misguided War on Terror that has brought us to our knees.

Really, and that's not hyperbole.

We are on our knees, carrying a world of debt on our shoulders! And this debt has destroyed the American Dream.

But there's hope!

A Trump presidency will restore hope in the American people as we restore the American Dream!

We are in this to win it!

We are in it to win for the American people!

I recently announced staff additions that are the continuation of our plan to have a strategic and significant presence across the country.

We are going to compete everywhere, and we are going to win because the American people have had enough of losing!

And I take strength from the Bible: "When a man's ways please the Lord, he maketh even his enemies to be at peace with him."

Hear that, Hillary Hippo Hips Hypocrite, you pathetic loser piece of human shit?

The Bushes, the Clintons, and Obama have done so much to destroy the hope and aspirations of the American people!

But despair ends!

The belief that the American Dream is history ends!

The American Dream will be restored, and we will not stop until the American Dream is within everyone's reach!

Make America Great Again!

Vote Trump.

11. We Need to Protect America as a Beacon of Freedom

Our leaders are stupid!

They are mistaken when they think that America can change its historic role in the world with no consequences.

For the entire world, America is the beacon of hope!

It is the land of opportunity! It is where you go to be free and to live free!

Then, suddenly, under the guise of "tolerance," "diversity," and "multiculturalism," we relinquish our historic role in civilizing the world!

Let me be clear!

Let me be perfectly clear!

Have you seen photographs of people arriving at Ellis Island?

Since the 19th century, millions of people have arrived at Ellis Island in New York Harbor to begin the process of *becoming* Americans.

There's a museum there on Ellis Island.

Look at the photographs!

Look at the photographs and what do you see?

You see boatloads of peasants!

They are forlorn, with all their earthly possessions with them, clutching the little money they have in their hands.

But they are coming to America because America is the future!

They are coming to America to escape whatever hellish land they are fleeing!

Frenchmen escaping the Reign of Terror! Irish escaping famine! Sicilians fleeing poverty!

It makes no difference where they originated from or what prompted their flight, they are coming to America to begin new lives.

But take a closer look at those pictures on display at Ellis Island.

What else do you see?

I'll tell you what you see: You see boatloads of stinking peasants, illiterate and destitute, backward and unsophisticated.

You see the scum of their homelands.

Let's face it!

The educated and prosperous didn't come to America—with rare exceptions, such as the White Russians fleeing the Bolshevik Revolution and, decades later, the Cuban middle class escaping Fidel Castro.

But everyone else?

They were destitute, illiterate, backward peasants!

Look at the pictures!

The huddled masses yearning to be free look like extras in a film about medieval serfs and oppressed proletariat!

But that's fine: America takes the bottom of the barrel.

Why?

Because America is where *peasants* come to become *humans!*

Humans!

America is where Neanderthals become proper members of Homo sapiens!

Multiculturalism wants to end that, so we have an America where there are clusters of oppressed communities of Neanderthals scattered around the country!

That's insane!

We need to go back to making immigrants into Americans! And our roots were imposing law and order on immigrants!

Welcome to America!

Take that basket off your heads! Take off those peasant rags and burn them!

Ladies, shave your legs and pluck your eyebrows! Gentlemen, shower with soap and visit the neighborhood barber!

Leave your peasant past behind!

Welcome to America, where we don't balance baskets on our heads, dress like serfs, or have self-esteem so low that we don't take pride in our appearance!

Welcome to America, where our daughters have the right to an education, are entitled to exercise their reproductive rights, and are free from being subjected to genital mutilation!

Welcome to America, where our sons are free to pursue education, live like free men, and where they will respect women.

That's how it's been throughout history: America renders *modern* the *backward*.

And there are certain rules about becoming modern human beings!

After you take the baskets off your heads, you burn your peasant rags, shower up, and get groomed! There are rules in America!

Rule #1: Learn English!

Rule #2: Abandon the Neanderthal practices of the Old Country.

What does Rule #2 mean?

It means that in America, our daughters are not kept illiterate!

It means that in America, our children decide whom they marry, not the parents!

It means that in America, there is no clitoral mutilation!

It means that in America, there is respect for the integrity of the individual and his or her self-determination!

Women have reproductive rights and men are not bound by tradition tied to the Neanderthal ways of the savage lands you abandoned on this journey across the ocean to become Americans!

This is how it's been done!

It's how it's been done—and how it's worked.

Until now.

Why?

Liberal Losers.

Liberal Losers, enamored by gaudy costumes of foreign lands and Zen practices, including yoga—which, by the way, I endorse—have gone overboard.

These guiding principles, enshrined in the photographs of the pathetic peasants arriving at Ellis Island with the hope, the dream, the desperate desire to become *Americans!*

Americans!

These are the principles that are being eroded under the false, bullshit god of multiculturalism.

These are values that are being destroyed by the liberal fascism of political correctness.

It is terrible, terrible, terrible to see America transformed into a place where, under the banner of tolerance, we now have to tolerate the intolerable: *The arrival of peasants who wish to remain peasants in our country, refusing to learn our language and assimilate.*

We call it "diversity," but what we're talking about is backwardness!

We are becoming a nation of peasants!

We are becoming a nation where peasants show up and, instead of becoming Americans, they are encouraged to remain peasants!

They want to balance baskets on their heads!

They want to keep dressing up like an ethnic holiday from hell!

They want to keep their daughters illiterate!

They want to order their sons who to marry!

They want to mutilate their daughter's clitoris and bully their wives into walking around in public dressed like black crows!

They want to preserve the Neanderthal ways of the Old Country from which they *fled!*

And this is not restricted to illiterate peasants alone.

When we have people come to our country who demand that we allow them the right to refuse to assimilate. They demand the right to continue practicing offensive traditions from the Dark Ages.

In many parts of the world, for instance, it's common for wealthy men to have more than one wife. In this country, only the Mormons believe that — and we are constantly prosecuting bigamists.

But what happens when we have a Saudi prince, Majed Abdulaziz Al-Saud, come to America and think he is *back* in Saudi Arabia — a backward, oppressive, despicable society where women cannot drive cars, are not allowed to be out in public without a male

112

escort, or exercise their reproductive rights.

Can you believe it?

Can you believe the United States is an ally of a country that runs like a medieval theocracy? In Saudi Arabia they execute teenagers by beheading them and then displaying their bodies, crucified, on public view!

Unbelievable! Unbelievable we even have diplomatic relations with such savages!

So, this Saudi prince shows up in America and thinks he can have his way with women in our country the way he has his way with women in his country.

And you know where this story goes: sexual assault.

He wants to have a harem of sex slaves in Beverly Hills!

I'm not making this up!

This Muslim Perv engages in sexual assaults so brazen, the cops are called in, and he's arrested.

Believe me, there's going to be some high-power corrupt deal in Washington, and this weak administration will cave in and let that Saudi Perv prince go.

"It will be a diplomatic incident if His Royal Highness is prosecuted for rape and abduction!" someone in the lame Obama administration will say.

This is what happens when we refuse to enforce assimilation as an integral part of immigration!

And this is crazy!

Give *me* a break! Give *America* a break!

We cannot keep America a modern society if we allow peasants from the world over to import their backwardness into America! We cannot allow rich perverts from oppressive countries to mistreat women in America the way they abuse women back home!

And this happens EVERYWHERE in America!

Don't believe me?

All you have to do is go to ANY college or university in this country and interview an ombudsman.

What will you find?

Any university that has foreign students will tell the same tale: Male students from oppressive lands hate the U.S. and can't wait to go back home; female students from those same countries love the U.S. and want to figure out how to stay!

Why?

Male students from oppressive countries are used to bullying and bossing their mothers, sisters, and aunts around. They hate the fact that women in the U.S. are free and independent; they can't be bossed around.

Female students from those same countries are overjoyed to be in a place where no man can bully or boss them. For the first time in their lives their fathers, uncles, or brothers can't tell them what to do—and they can uncover their heads, drive cars, and go out and about as they see fit.

That's the clash of cultures!

That's why we have to end the bullshit of multiculturalism. It creates a society where many levels of oppression, repression, and exploitation can take place.

We cannot have the savage traditions of a Neanderthal past take root in America, whether it is an illiterate peasant from Bangladesh who wants to mutilate his daughter's clitoris, or a Saudi prince who wants to have a harem of sex slaves in Beverly Hills!

Oh, trust me!

It may look hip in the pages of *National Geographic*, all these ethnic women all over the place balancing baskets on their heads, but trust me!

It's not!

Ann Coulter is right when she says—*of the bullshit of multiculturalism*—that we are well on our way to making America into a Third-World Hellhole!

Ann Coulter is right about that: Diversity is a smokescreen for the continued oppression of women on America soil!

Let me tell you something about Ann! She's gorgeous! She's

brilliant! She's a Nine!

Hear that, Heidi Klum?

But better than being a Nine, Ann doesn't take any shit from anybody.

Did you know?

Did you know she went to Cornell? And did you know that at Cornell she used to hang out with the guys at Alpha Delta Phi?

It's true. Those fine young men taught her that *every* woman in this country has the right to be respected and that men have the obligation to treat women with respect—and as their equals, even fat pigs like Rosie O'Donnell.

You could say that the guys from Cornell's Alpha Delta Phi taught Ann Coulter to have *the balls* that she has when she takes on Liberal Losers who are trying to make this country like every other *wretched* place on earth where women are forced to balance baskets on their heads, dress up like black crows, and be subjected to genital mutilation!

And the guys from Alpha Delta Phi *also* taught Ann Coulter how to make the perfect martini—which is a tradition at Cornell since E. B. White taught there, between martinis—making *perfect* martinis!

And I make this compliment as a man who doesn't drink!

Except on special occasions! And yes, when I am elected, I will have a martini with Ann Coulter!

That said, I stand with Ann Coulter and make you the promise that America will not become the Land of Oppressed Women and Cowering Peasants!

I!

Will!

Not!

Let!

That!

Happen!

I will not let that happen!

Immigrants must leave their peasant past at the door!

115

Do I have disdain for backward societies?

You bet I do!

I mean, even immigrants realize they're coming from inferior societies.

Let's face it; an immigrant is a person who is LEAVING a place!

Why are they leaving?

Because it sucks! That's why they're leaving!

They are leaving societies that suck and societies where they are losers and they are coming to America!

Believe me; Queen Elizabeth II has no desire to be an immigrant to the United States! She's more than happy to live in Buckingham Palace!

But for the rest of the world?

Yes, they are leaving a place that SUCKS, and they are coming to America, a BETTER place.

And almost *every* immigrant is *leaving* a society that is *oppressive* and that *sucks*.

In fact, the more likely a woman is to balance a basket of anything on her head, the more likely she is to be shackled to a backward society where she does not have access to an education, have a say in whom she marries, or have any reproductive rights at all!

The more likely she is to balance a basket of anything on her head, the more oppressed she is!

And we want that?

Of course not!

Do we want these bullshit liberals telling us that peasants can come to America and keep practicing despicable cavemen traditions?

No!

America is not a collection of "independent" communities where savage traditions invented by Neanderthals are still practiced.

I live in New York.

New York has the potential to be the greatest city in the world. But it isn't.

Why?

Because New York is awash in Third World peasants living in poverty—and encouraged to remain outside the mainstream of American society by Liberal Losers who encourage them to keep practicing traditions that made them into impoverished peasants in the first place!

Give *me* a break! Give *America* a break!

We need an educated workforce that speaks English!

We need people who believe in the future—and are not beholden to the past!

We have, in New York City, clusters of people who believe that girls don't have the right to an education. We have, in New York City, communities of losers who disown their children if they are gay or lesbian. We have, in New York City, zip codes inhabited by Neanderthals who want to practice female genital mutilation and tell their sons whom to marry.

We have, in New York City, peasants *remaining* peasants!

This is an outrage!

This is un-American!

This ends!

Welcome to America, where we speak English!

Welcome to America, where your daughter will get an education and your son will be free to marry whom he wants!

Welcome to America, where you will not take a knife to your daughter's clitoris and you will not stand in the way of your son pursuing his dreams!

And if you don't like it, get on the next flight back to Oppressivestan!

And, believe me, Oppressivestan is oppressive indeed!

So, I want to talk about the oppression of women.

I love women! I respect women! I cherish women! I love, respect, and cherish women!

My daughter Ivanka is pregnant!

I'm so happy for her—and for me.

117

And I can tell you that I don't care if her baby is a boy or a girl! I want that baby to have the entire world available to him or her! I really do.

And because I want my grandson or grandchild to have every opportunity possible, I want him or her to live in a society that protects its citizens from peasant backwardness.

What do I mean?

I mean that societies have the right to have rules—take it or leave it.

For example, most modern societies have decided that, when you are in public, there are things we *don't* want to see and things we *do* want to see.

And we have laws to that effect.

We don't, for example, want to see your privates.

End of debate. Really. End of debate.

We just don't want to see your privates in public. If you want to be a home nudist or go to a naturist community, that's fine.

But if you're walking down Fifth Avenue on your way from Trump Tower to Rockefeller Center naked, you're going to be arrested for indecent exposure.

It's that simple.

If you want to live in public naked, then go to one of the communities in the Amazon where they're okay with public nudity. Or join the people in Papua New Guinea where they walk around naked. Or go to live with the Nuer people, the Nilotic tribe in Africa, where they're naked all the time. I mean, these are societies where everyone lives like that show on the Discovery Channel, *Naked and Afraid.*

But if you want to live in America, it's a different story.

In America, we've decided that we don't want to see penises or vaginas in public—breasts are different.

Why?

Because the courts have ruled that if men are allowed to go topless, so can women. That's why we have the Desnudas—young women wearing body paint instead of tops—pose for pictures with tourists in Times Square.

But anyway, in America, no penises or vaginas on view in public!

That's just the way it is, and I think just about everyone agrees that's a good rule.

Now, at the same time that we've decided what we *don't* want to see, we have also decided what we *do* want to see: *Your smile!*

It's that simple.

We want to see your smile.

And because we want to see people's smiles, we want faces uncovered.

You can't walk into a bank wearing a ski mask without alarming bank employees. You can't walk into an airport terminal wearing a motorcycle helmet without causing concern. And you can't walk around America wearing a burka—*a sign of misogynist oppression of women*—under the guise of "religious" freedom.

If you want to walk around dressed like a black crow, go back to Oppressivestan.

Head coverings, like scarves or hijabs, do not hide your smile.

But burkas do!

And before I'm accused of being a bigot, let me point out that other countries around the world—*other modern countries with liberal values*—agree with me.

France has banned burkas in public.

Catalonia in Spain has banned anyone from wearing ski masks, motorcycle helmets, and burkas in public buildings.

Even the European Court of Human Rights recognizes the right of European countries to ban burkas—and tacitly accepts that any religion that imposes a burka on a woman is misogynist.

America cannot become a savage Third-World country where clusters of people are free to live in the past, with backward practices that oppress women!

And this applies to all kinds of crazy, bullshit backwardness!

It applies to Amish Christians who take their kids out of school, condemning them to lives of ignorance. Or Hasidic Jews, who disown their sons if they happen to be gay. Or fundamentalist Muslims, who insist on forcing women to walk around America dressed like black crows.

This is not what America is about!

This is not who we are as a people!

As president, I will not allow clusters of peasants—*Neanderthal thinkers*—to impose "traditional" values that oppress others.

And that's a serious problem.

The Loser Leftists who champion multiculturalism are hypocrites.

Why?

Because they are condescending, smug know-it-alls!

Why do I say that?

Because they pretend to be *arbiters* of what is *acceptable* and what is *not acceptable*.

Here's an example.

Let us say that a boat shows up at Ellis Island and peasants disembark. And these peasants want to live as they did in the Old Country.

And their "traditional" way of life includes, 1) keeping their daughters illiterate, and 2) balancing a basket of rocks on their heads.

Do they get to keep their values?

I don't think anyone would agree that we should smile, nod our heads, and go along with their savage tradition of keeping their daughters illiterate.

We would *all* demand that their daughters go to school—and we would use the law to make them send their daughters to school if they refused!

But under the *pretense* of multiculturalism, there are those who say they should be free to walk around balancing baskets of rocks on their heads.

Or wear stupid clothes like a *National Geographic* magazine spread, or whatever.

Well, who gets to decide which "traditional" value is acceptable and which is not?

What if these peasant savages engaged in female circumcision? What if they stoned gay sons?

Once they step foot onto American soil, we have a right to say, "Keeping girls out of school is wrong!"

No Malala martyrs in America!

So, we *can* say "NO!" to "traditional" values that are barbaric!

Multiculturalism that oppresses people is not the kind of "diversity" that will be "celebrated" in America!

Why?

Because in America we don't balance baskets on our heads, disown our gay children, stone dissenters, or engage in any other Neanderthal practice.

I repeat, America is where peasants come to become human beings!

And I repeat, the hoax of "multiculturalism" has been used by the Left to encourage cultural practices that oppress people within our borders!

We cannot be a nation that turns a blind eye to Neanderthal bigots banishing their gay sons, or slicing up their daughter's clitorises, or using religion to have harems, or molesting children.

Are we going to have "traditional" Muslims behead people in their community as part of law enforcement? Are we going to allow Hasidic Jews to stone adulterers to death? Are we going to tolerate fringe Christian sects that deny their children lifesaving medicine? Are we going to let Mexican peasants rip the hearts of sacrifices to their sun god?

America, I repeat, is where savages are civilized!

And the hoax of multiculturalism prevents us from transforming peasants into people.

Women have dreamed of coming to America to shave their legs and pluck their eyebrows—in defiance of their parents. Men have dreamed of coming to America to wash their body odor away, shave their faces, and marry the girl they truly, madly, deeply love!

And, quite frankly, if an immigrant woman is hot, after she shaves her legs—and armpits—she might consider getting a bikini wax.

Just saying.

But, grooming apart, how do you think I feel to live in a city where Mexican peasants are walking around speaking Zapotec, balancing baskets on their heads, and are clueless about the concept of kindergarten for their anchor babies?

How do you think I feel to live in city where repressive Hasidic jerks disown gay sons and bully their daughters into prearranged marriages?

How do you think I feel to live in a city where "conservative" Muslim assholes demand their wives walk around town dressed like black crows and want to take knives to their daughters' clitorises?

This has got to stop!

We are one country!

Trust me, my wife—who, by the way is a Ten—came to America and went through all the steps of becoming an American.

Did you hear that, Heidi Klum?

A woman can be an immigrant from Europe, become an American citizen, give birth, and still be a Ten!

I repeat: Gay Tim Gunn guy on *Project Runway* isn't doing you any favors by not helping you camouflage. That's why you're no longer a Ten.

And I know about Tens!

My beautiful wife, Melania, is a Ten. And more than that: Melania learned English, which she speaks far better than that apologist for illegals, Jorge Ramos!

And she went through each and every step to become a naturalized American citizen!

If we are to remain a *beacon of freedom*, we cannot become a *bastion of Neanderthals* from a prehistoric past!

Multiculturalism wants an America filled with peasants, peons, serfs, and voiceless women!

We cannot have that!

We must have an America where everyone is a citizen, equal under the law, and living free from the oppressions of the past!

Make America Great Again!

Vote Trump.

12. We Must Restore Our Moral Standing in the World

Our leaders are stupid!

We are living in a time when gestures are considered more important than accomplishments.

Look at our president, Obama.

He believes—wrongly, I might add—that his "legacy" will be anything but disaster. In fact, Obama's foreign policy legacy is only slightly less terrible than Bush II's, who made the blunder of the century when he invaded Iraq.

Obama has not been able to do anything to straighten out Bush II's monumental blunder. We left Iraq stupidly. We remain in Afghanistan stupidly. And we lost Syria to Russia stupidly.

Stupid is as Obama does. Stupid is as Secretary of State Hillary Clinton did.

As a result, do you see what's going on in the world?

ISIS is beheading people, overrunning entire nations. Iran is swooping in to take over Iraq. China is getting all the oil it wants—which should rightfully be America's!

Jordan is drowning in a sea of refugees—and Syria is a disaster!

Syria!

Syria!

ISIS is trying to take over the country. Assad, whom we loved until we hated him, is besieged. We're supposed to be backing the opponents—but no one understands who the opponents really are that are fighting Assad.

Our president declared a line that couldn't be crossed, and when it was crossed, we did nothing.

In this mess, Putin has stepped in.

So now we have a situation where Russia is bombing Assad's opponents to prop up Assad. We're bombing ISIS to stop that threat.

We're not supporting Assad's opponents—whom we really haven't vetted—and Assad is being strengthened by the Russians.

And Russia authorized the deployment of ground forces in Syria.

A chaotic situation is now more dangerous.

The world, under this terrible, terrible, terrible administration, is getting more dangerous.

The Russian foray into Syria is a terrible escalation, one that threatens a direct, if accidental, confrontation with the United States.

Russia, by the way, is increasing its sphere of influence in the Middle East by propping up the Assad regime. In the same way that Putin annexed Crimea in Ukraine, this adventure into Syria will cement Moscow's power in Syria, which straddles Iraq and Turkey.

Guess what, Kenyan Socialist?

Guess what, failed Secretary of State Hillary Hippo Hips Hypocrite?

Putin was positioning Russia as a superpower once more—while Obama golfed and Hillary emailed!

To these disasters, add that terrible, terrible Iran deal, which will give Iran billions and billions of dollars.

Israeli Prime Minister Benjamin Netanyahu stared down the General Assembly at the United Nations to shame those who support a deal that sells out Israel and strengthens the Islamic Republic of Iranian Terrorists.

Unbelievable!

Can it get worse?

With Obama, the answer is, OF COURSE!

What the Democrats are afraid of is that history will show that this president's pathetic inaction led to the rise of ISIS.

Well, it did.

We drew a red line in Ukraine. The Russians crossed it. We did nothing.

That showed the world we're weak.

We drew a red line in Syria. Assad crossed it. We did nothing.

125

That showed the world we're weak.

Now, Putin and Assad have teamed up.

Russia is bombing the hell out of our so-called allies in Syria, and we're doing nothing. ISIS is moving further to take over Iraq and Syria.

And, back in Afghanistan, the Taliban are back!

The Taliban are back! The Taliban are back!

And the Taliban are savages who blow things up! They're the savages who shoot young girls in the head on their way to school! They're the savages who finance their terrorism by selling heroin to drug addicts all over Europe!

That's how they keep girls illiterate! They shoot them in the head if they're walking to school!

Malala!

There are millions of young girls like Malala—attacked for wanting to learn!

They're savages, these radical Muslims!

They blow up monuments.

Do you know how that offends me?

I *build* things! It breaks my heart when others *destroy* things!

But do you know what's worse that all this?

It is the moral depravity of this administration.

Before I get to that, I need to talk about Pope John Paul II.

He was a great man. In fact, he's been canonized by the Catholic Church.

If that's the case, then we can say we lived in the presence of a saint.

But even saints aren't perfect.

John Paul II's one failing was his refusal to believe that Satan had infiltrated the Church in the form of sexual predators.

Hundreds, if not thousands, of priests around the world sexually abused boys and girls.

The Vatican failed to act to stop this—and this legacy of child abuse and the damage inflicted on tens of thousands of children around the world will take a *generation* for the Catholic Church to overcome. Pope Francis recognizes as much—by the way, when he was on his papal visit, he met with individuals who had been victimized by sexual predators hiding within the ranks of the Catholic Church.

What does this have to do with Obama's legacy?

Everything!

I mean everything!

The Pentagon, under the Obama administration, has provided institutional protection to sexual predators, child rapists, and child molesters!

Unbelievable!

I'm a father! I'm a grandfather!

You cannot believe the outrage I feel knowing that American taxpayers have been—under this corrupt, immoral, and depraved administration—harboring sexual predators!

As an American I am enraged that this has been going on!

Is it any wonder we have lost our moral standing in the world when we have a president who has no moral compass?

You do know the Nobel Peace Prize committee now regrets having awarded Barack Obama the Peace Prize, don't you?

Even as I speak, the Pentagon is in the process of discharging courageous American patriots who have defended the weakest among us: children.

Lance Corporal Gregory Buckley refused to obey an *immoral* order to look the other way while Afghan child molesters sexually assaulted children.

This is how the *New York Times* reported this outrage: "Rampant sexual abuse of children has long been a problem in Afghanistan, particularly among armed commanders who dominate much of the rural landscape and can bully the population. The practice is called *bacha bazi*, literally 'boy play,' and American soldiers and Marines have been instructed not to intervene—in some cases, not even when their Afghan allies have abused boys on military bases, according to

127

interviews and court records."

Buckley's father told reporters his son confided: "At night we can hear them screaming, but we're not allowed to do anything about it."

What?

We can do nothing about a man *raping* a child in a place where the U.S. *military* has control?

Outrageous!

But the Pentagon, under orders from the Obama administration, let child rapists rape all they want and child molesters molest all they want—all for political expediency!

My fellow Americans, when did the United States become a force of evil in the world?

I want to know!

When did we lose our moral compass in such a despicable way?

Listen to this! Listen to the *New York Times*: "The American policy of nonintervention is intended to maintain good relations with the Afghan police and militia units the United States has trained to fight the Taliban. It also reflects a reluctance to impose cultural values in a country where pederasty is rife, particularly among powerful men, for whom being surrounded by young teenagers can be a mark of social status."

What?

We have become an outlaw nation! We have become a presence of evil in the world!

What do you think those children will think of us?

Is it any wonder we are hated?

Is it any wonder radicals around the world want to fly passenger planes into our skyscrapers?

This is what Dan Quinn, a former Special Forces captain, who pummeled a pervert who had a boy chained to his bed as a sex slave, said: "The reason we were here is because we heard the terrible things the Taliban were doing to people, how they were taking away human rights. But we were putting people into power who would do things that were worse than the Taliban did—that was something village elders voiced to me."

Barack Obama believes his foreign policy legacy will be the Iran nuclear deal.

He's wrong!

He will be remembered as the American president who punished American soldiers who fought to prevent a child rapist from keeping a child chained to a bed to be used as a sex slave!

We can have no moral standing in the world when we have an immoral president!

And, may I remind you, this policy was endorsed by Secretary of State Hillary Clinton—who, by the way, is the worst secretary of state in the history of the world!

Understandable: If Hillary didn't give a fuck about Bill sexually assaulting Monica Lewinsky, why should she give a fuck about our military protecting child rapists in Afghanistan?

Now, before anyone objects, saying that Bill, that Perv, didn't assault Monica because Monica "consented," well, let me just point out the disparate power positions—*an unpaid intern versus the most powerful man in the world!*

I submit that the nature of her "consent" is dubious.

You don't want me to start quoting from Andrea Dworkin's book, *Intercourse*, do you?

Because I will!

And I know you don't want me to start quoting from that disgusting dead fat pig's book that championed misandry!

What is not in dispute is that under the Barack Obama–Hillary Clinton regime, America has allowed the systematic *rape* of boys and girls with complete impunity!

This is a bigger scandal than the Perv priests in the Catholic Church!

I am the *only* candidate willing to speak the truth to the world: *America, under this administration, has become a force for evil!*

I'm ashamed! I'm ashamed and horrified that this is

129

happening—and I think that every decent American is ashamed as well.

And our men and women in uniform—not unlike German soldiers who were ordered to turn a blind eye to the horrors of Nazi Germany—are now being forced into becoming *unwilling* accomplices in the systematic *sexual exploitation* of children by monsters acting under the *protection* of the *Pentagon*.

Outrage!

Want more outrage?

Do you know what happened to Lance Corporal Gregory Buckley?

The Afghans, not knowing he was ordered to look the other way as their children were being raped and sexually assaulted under the protection of the U.S. military, killed him!

The Afghans *killed* Buckley because they believed that American Marines *condoned* the *rape* of their children!

Unbelievable!

This is what Buckley's father said: "As far as the young boys are concerned, the Marines are allowing it to happen and so they're guilty by association. They don't know our Marines are sick to their stomachs."

An American patriot was *murdered* by the parents of raped children, who mistakenly believed that Americans condone child rape!

Outrage! Outrage! Outrage!

And it gets worse!

For those American patriots to defy the immoral orders of Obama's Pentagon, there is retaliation. Captain Dan Quinn along with Sergeant First Class Charles Martland, who also pummeled a child rapist, were forced out of the military!

Both Quinn and Martland were Green Berets on their second tour in northern Kunduz Province when they acted to stop the rape of a teenage girl.

And for that, they're forced out of the military.

Outrage on top of outrage!

And Obama's moral depravity doesn't stop with the U.S. military.

Did you know that during his time in office, hundreds and hundreds of American sexual predators have made their way to Mexico?

Did you know that Mexico is emerging as a sex-tourism destination that rivals Thailand?

And it is in the sleepy, peaceful cities—*where it is least expected*—that American sexual predators are setting up base.

I think everyone in the U.S. has heard of Cancún, the incredibly successful resort in Mexico. In fact, did you know there are more flights from the U.S. to Cancún than there are to any other resort in the Caribbean?

It's true.

But near Cancún is the city of Mérida, which is a sizable city of about a million people.

Get ready to be shocked: This city, which you probably never heard of before, has become, under the morally depraved Obama administration, the center for American pedophiles down in Mexico!

All you have to do is go to Google and search for "Mérida," "American," and "murdered," and up comes a list of Americans killed by Mexican teenagers those American perverts were trying to rape.

So what we have here is the systematic sexual exploitation of children around the world with the blessing of the Obama administration.

Closer to home, American pedophiles are running amok in Mexico, while the FBI does nothing—which, by the way, it can *under the concept of universal jurisdiction*—to bring these sex criminals to justice. And on the other side of the world, the U.S. Pentagon has been ordered to protect child molesters and sexual predators.

Unbelievable!

Is it any wonder we are hated? Is it any wonder the world looks at us with disgust? Is it any wonder our moral standing in the world has crumbled because of the Obama administration? Is it any wonder the Nobel Peace Prize committee regrets having given Obama the Nobel Peace Prize?

Unbelievable!

I can assure you that this immoral administration's depraved policies end when I'm elected!

It's only fair that if we will make Mexico pay to build the wall, then the U.S. will pay to repatriate the hundreds and hundreds of American pedophiles preying on children south of the border.

We will swoop in to protect children wherever we have jurisdiction—either through the Pentagon in Afghanistan or, through universal jurisdiction, which holds American citizens accountable for sex crimes against children anywhere in the world.

You can count on that!

Do you know how we also restore our moral standing the world?

By keeping our word!

By keeping our promises!

If America does not keep its word and honor its promises, no one will believe us.

Well, guess what?

Secretary of State Hillary Clinton—who, by the way, was the worst secretary of state in U.S. history—went along with the Obama administration to *betray* the Iraqis and Afghans who have helped us.

When Bush II launched that disastrous invasion of Iraq and occupation of Afghanistan, America needed Iraqi and Afghan interpreters and translators.

We gave them our word and made the promise that, when we left, we would give them visas to come to the U.S.

Why?

Because by helping us, they were putting themselves at risk.

So we have Iraqi and Afghan interpreters and translators willing to help us—*risking their lives*—because they *believed* that Americans are people of their *word* who would keep their *promises.*

Guess what?

When Obama pulled out of Iraq and began to leave Afghanistan, we betrayed the Iraqis and Afghans.

The same way we betrayed so many Vietnamese who believed in us a generation ago, Obama has now betrayed thousands and thousands of Iraqis and Afghans.

Since 2007 the U.S. has issued only 14,000 visas to Iraqi and Afghan interpreters and translators. There are more than 13,000 waiting.

Hillary Hippo Hips Hypocrite has no problem breaking our word — probably because, let's face it, she didn't give a fuck when Bill broke his marital vows to her, right?

And this is a matter of life and death: Every 36 hours, one of the interpreters or translators who worked for us, believed in us, and that Obama betrayed, is murdered!

They are being murdered because they are seen as collaborators with the United States.

I'm ashamed!

Aren't you ashamed that we have betrayed those who put their trust in us?

Unbelievable!

That's not the America I want!

That's not the America the world needs!

We will keep our word and keep our promises.

The Age of American Betrayal under Barack Obama and Hillary Clinton ends when I'm sworn in!

The world and the American people know that I don't have the blood of innocents on my hands, innocents betrayed by Barack Obama and Hillary Clinton!

You can be sure that I will restore our moral standing in the world!

Day 1 in office, the Pentagon is ordered to treat any sex crime against a child that occurs where the U.S. military has jurisdiction as a war crime!

Day 1 in office, the Pentagon is ordered to arrest all child rapists, child molesters, and sexual predators preying on children where the U.S. military has jurisdiction!

Day 1 in office, the FBI will be ordered to prepare to arrest American pedophiles preying on children throughout the world!

Day 1 in office, I will order that Gregory Buckley, Dan Quinn, and Charles Martland be awarded the Presidential Medal of Freedom!

Day 1 in office, the moral depravity of the Obama administration—which has empowered, protected, and cultivated sex crimes against children—ends!

America cannot be great again if we have this legacy of protecting sex crimes against children!

Make America Great Again!

Vote Trump.

13. Why I Don't Need the Latino Vote, but I Want the Latino Vote

Our leaders are stupid!

Our leaders lie to the American people when they tell voters that all votes count equally.

Trust me, trust me on this one: All votes are equal, but some are more equal than others!

Why?

Because of the Electoral College!

Did you know?

Americans do *not* vote for president because there is no *direct* election of the president. Americans vote for *electors* to the Electoral College.

There is no direct election of the president in the United States. *No one* votes *for* president!

Everyone votes for a slate of electors who assemble in the Electoral College. These electors, who consist of 538 men and women, are the people who, in fact, elect the president and vice president. Of course most people don't realize this and actually believe their vote counts for something.

Unless you happen to live in one of the few states—the so-called "swing states"—voting in presidential elections is, to be honest, a waste of time.

The swing states are: Colorado, Iowa, Florida, Minnesota, Nevada, New Hampshire, North Carolina, Ohio, Pennsylvania, Virginia, and Wisconsin.

If you don't live in these states, voting in 2016 is of virtually no consequence. Of course many people feel differently and believe it's their civic duty to vote.

That's fine.

Go ahead.

Vote.

But let's be honest: It won't make a difference.

Remember Andy Rooney?

"I have a message for the 100 million Americans who didn't care enough about our democracy to vote last time. Good! And, please, do us all a favor. Don't vote next time, either. If you don't care enough about the issues, I don't want you canceling out my vote with your vote," Andy Rooney implored his fellow Americans on *60 Minutes*.

He thought I was a great guy, and I thought he was a swell man.

Of course Rooney was criticizing the public's apathy, where civic duties do not include caring about public policy issues. Rooney raised valid points, but ignorant or apathetic voters don't care about the discussion I'm making here on the futility of voting in presidential elections.

The misgivings I have are about the nature of *honesty*.

In fact, it's because it's *dishonest* to pretend to have a democracy where it is *one-person, one-vote* when that's not the case. Because there is no direct election of the president, the popular vote does *not* determine who wins and who loses.

I have the figures here!

Listen to this and be shocked: In 2000, 100,405,100 votes were cast in the presidential election. Here is a breakdown of which candidate received how many of these votes:

Al Gore:	50,999,897
George W. Bush	50,456,002
Ralph Nader	2,882,955
Pat Buchanan	448,895

The remaining votes were cast for other candidates, including Harry Browne of the Libertarian Party (384,431 votes), Howard Phillips of the Constitution Party (98,020 votes), and John Hagelin of the Natural Law Party (83,714 votes). The remaining votes went to minor candidates or write-in names.

136

If Al Gore received 543,895 *more* votes than George W. Bush, and if the United States were a true democracy, why was George W. Bush declared the winner?

The Electoral College!

The distribution of the popular vote among various states resulted in a *distortion* of actual votes cast by members of the Electoral College. This resulted in George W. Bush *winning* the Electoral College vote and Al Gore *losing*.

When the Electoral College vote goes one way and the national popular vote goes another way, it is called a *failure*. The *failure* rate, in which the presidential candidate with the most popular votes *loses* the election, is one in 14.

Now, listen up, Jorge Ramos and every other Latino critic: *This is huge!*

Under the current Electoral College regime, the minimum number of electors from each state and the District of Columbia stands at three, regardless of how many people actually live in these states and the District of Columbia. If one considers the 2008 populations census figures, Wyoming, with a population of only 532,668, had three electoral votes. This is an average of 177,556 voters per electoral vote. Compared to the 2008 national average, a Wyoming resident's vote was "worth" 318 percent more than the national population vis-à-vis the number each electoral votes averages of the nation's population. Other states with far lower voters per electoral vote include Vermont (273%), North Dakota (264%), Alaska (247%), Rhode Island (215%), and South Dakota (211%), and, of course, the District of Columbia (286%).

What does this mean?

It means that the Electoral College is the most sophisticated system ever created to suppress the votes of people of color!

Yes, that's what it does.

A white voter in Wyoming can cancel out THREE votes of people of color—Latinos, blacks, Asians—in California.

A white voter in Vermont can almost cancel out THREE votes of people of color in Texas!

And so forth and so on.

WHITE voters in rural states can cancel out anywhere between TWO and THREE votes that Latinos cast in California, Texas, Arizona, or Florida.

It's that simple because it's math!

And that's how WHITE voters canceled out the 543,895 MORE votes cast by people of color—in the WRONG states—for Al Gore.

Think about that: 543,895 more people of color throughout the country voted for Al Gore—and, yet, Al Gore lost the election!

I can have hundreds of thousands of Latinos voting against me—and I, too, can win the election without a problem!

Latinos votes don't matter in presidential elections because of the Electoral College!

I don't *need* Latino votes because there aren't Latinos in the states where voting really, really, really counts: Wyoming, South Dakota, Alaska, and so on!

The Electoral College, quite frankly, tears that principle of equality asunder. A vote in Wyoming is worth three times as much as a vote cast by a voter in Texas. In consequence, it takes *three* Texas residents to vote for candidate X to cancel the single vote cast by a resident in Wyoming for candidate Y.

The reverse is also true, of course. A Wyoming resident's vote carries three times the weight of a Texas voter's vote. The same Electoral College "privilege" is afforded residents of Vermont, North Dakota, and the District of Columbia, whose votes are worth almost three times those of Texas voters.

And when you throw demographics into place, it's indisputable: WHITE voters in these states CANCEL out multiple votes that LATINOS cast in California, Texas, Arizona, and Nevada.

That's the way it—the Electoral College suppresses the votes of people of color, pure and simple.

The truth is that, *electorally-speaking*, Latinos can go fuck themselves!

138

Their votes don't matter! Their votes didn't matter in 2000, and their votes won't matter in 2016!

I didn't invent this system, but it's going to work for me—and work for me *huge!*

Then again, let's face it: When Latinos vote, Latinos vote stupid!

That explains Gavin Newsom's political career: *Latinos voting stupid!*

That explains Nancy Pelosi, that racist piece of human shit, being in Congress: *Latinos voting stupid!*

That explains that terrible disaster Kenyan Socialist Obama being in the White House: *Latinos voting stupid!*

So, come November 2016, there's a chance for Latinos to *redeem* themselves: *They can vote for me.*

And they will!

Why?

Because I speak for the Silent Hispanic Majority in this country, the Latino media do not!

Listen closely: There are about 45 million Hispanics in this country—at least that's what the Census Bureau will report when they conduct the next census in a few years.

And there are disagreements over the number of illegals in the country. The truth is no one really knows the exact number. I've heard 10 million, and I've heard as high as 20 million.

So let's split the difference and say there are 15 million people living illegally in our country.

So, if there are 45 million Hispanics in the country and 15 million of them are illegals, I'm speaking for the 30 million LEGAL Hispanics.

These 30 million people are the *Silent Hispanic Majority.*

And my critics, my critics in the Latino media—like Jorge Ramos—are advocating on behalf of the ILLEGAL Latino *Minority!*

It's true!

The *minority* of Hispanics in this country are *illegal.*

I speak for the *Legal* Latino Majority.

Jorge Ramos speaks for the *Illegal* Latino Minority.

That's what it comes down to: *The Legal Latino Majority versus the Illegal Latino Minority*.

Guess which one gets all the media coverage?

Not the Silent Hispanic Majority!

Of course not! People doing the right thing and obeying the law is not newsworthy!

But lawbreakers who want amnesty, there's media whore Jorge Ramos running after them with his Univision television crew!

"Oh, *pobrecito*," that pathetic apologist for criminals says. "You entered the U.S. illegally, were deported, snuck back in, raped, murdered an innocent American citizen, and they refuse to serve you gluten-free bread at the maximum security prison? This is a violation of your human rights! I'm outraged!"

It gets worse! Yes, it gets worse!

While Latino Losers in the media vilify me for standing up for law and order, they forget that the Silent Hispanic Majority backs me.

Would it surprise you to know that 65 percent of Hispanics believe in enforcing immigration laws?

Sixty-five percent of Hispanics support "Enforcement First" when it comes to immigration.

Hispanics support enforcing the immigration laws of the land, by a margin of 65 percent to 35 percent. This poll was taken by John McLaughlin and it's widely available—but the Latino media ignores it.

And there's more support for my position.

Did you know that by a margin of 56 percent to 40 percent Hispanics oppose allowing illegals to get federal benefits—from food stamps to welfare?

And the Silent Hispanic Majority believes that there should be employment verification to determine if a job applicant is a lawful resident. They also believe illegals should not cut in front of the line when trying to get back in the U.S.

Legal Hispanics are *tougher* than non-Hispanics on the illegals than I am!

This is the true, honest, and poll-certified position of the Silent Hispanic Majority.

Do you see? Do you see a pattern?

Thirty-five percent of Latinos are opposed to me, but 65 percent agree with me.

That means that the ILLEGAL Latinos are against me and the LEGAL Latinos are for me!

But you wouldn't know any of that by listening to Jorge Ramos!

He wants you to believe that ALL Latinos hate me.

Well, guess what?

Illegals can't vote!

I want the 65 percent of Latinos—the *Silent Hispanic Majority*—to vote for me! I want *their* support!

And I *have* their support!

Where is Jorge Ramos reporting on the anger, the outrage, the fury of LEGAL Hispanics who are forced to live under the "Cloud of Suspicion" because of all the illegals around us.

In fact, Jorge Ramos admitted to the *New Yorker* magazine that he's not interested in journalism, but pontificating.

I have it right here. This is what he said: "Normally, I'd just have a ten-second question prepared. But this is not normal. Here I have to make a statement, as an indignant immigrant. Tell him that Latinos despise him. And then I have to ask a question, as a journalist, if he'll let me."

Can you believe it? Can you believe it?

This was his game plan in Iowa when he wouldn't sit down, shut up, and wait his turn.

It was *my* press conference, not *his*. I was the one making a statement, not reporters in the audience!

And what was the statement that he wanted to say to me? He wanted to tell me to my face that Latinos despise me.

Really?

The Silent Hispanic Majority—*65 percent of them*—agree with me.

They—65 percent of Hispanics—don't despise me! They're *with* me!

I repeat: Jorge Ramos speaks for the *Illegal Latino Minority*—the ones who can't vote and the ones who have no right to be in our country!

Unbelievable!

And while I want to restore law and order, do you know what Mexico's president is doing?

He flies to New York to address the United Nations.

Do you know what Mexico's president, Enrique Peña Nieto, said at the United Nations?

I have it here!

He said, "*En todos los continentes, en todas las latitudes, los migrantes viven historias de riesgo, de rechazo, discriminación y abuso. Estas condiciones se agravan cuando por ignorancia, mala fe, racismo o mero oportunismo político, los inmigrantes y sus hijos son estigmatizados y responsabilizados de las dificultades propias de los países de destino.*"

Do you know what that means?

Do you give a fuck about what that means?

I know I don't!

And since these are two complete sentences in Spanish, I doubt Low-Energy Jeb Bush would know either—since he speaks Spanish only in *six-second sound bites* for Univision. And to order value meals at Taco Bell while on his low-energy, pathetic noncampaign trail.

But Mexico's president at the U.N.?

I know I don't give a fuck what Mexico's president said at the United Nations—which, by the way, is across the street from one of my buildings, the Trump World Tower, which *soars* over the United Nations, offering sweeping views of the East River.

It's a gorgeous building, and I'm sure Presidente Wetbacko saw it as his limousine pulled up to the *Naciones Unidas*.

Yes, that's right: I have a building that towers over the United Nations!

All I know is that it doesn't matter what Mexico's president said because there is nothing he can say that will prevent America from deporting Mexican illegals who are in our country!

They are going back!

They have to go back!

They are here illegally and we are a nation of laws!

There is nothing Mexico's president can say that will stop the Trump administration from enforcing the immigration laws of the United States of America!

The illegals are gone!

Now, that means that if someone is here illegally, but is a productive member of society—has a job, pays taxes, owns a business, has formed a family—they will not be *banned* for life from coming back.

That's not compassionate, and we are a compassionate nation.

So, yes, they have to go back—and THEN apply to return LEGALLY!

They have to go back and *then* apply—just like the other 30 million Hispanics who are in the U.S. legally—because they came to this country following our laws or they were born here to legal parents!

It's that simple!

Enrique Peña Nieto at the United Nations?

Ridiculous!

Hey, Mexican asshole—where are those missing students, you corrupt thief? You're a fucking piece of human shit!

Instead of wasting everyone's time at the United Nations you should be looking for those missing students—that's what your people want you to do!

Have you looked to see if those missing students are in one of the *dozen* closets in that huge mansion you and your corrupt wife got from your cronies?

Maybe the missing students are somewhere in that palatial mansion of yours, you corrupt piece of human shit!

Go back to Mexico—and take Jorge Ramos with you!

And take the other 15 million illegals with you as well, you loser!

Low-Energy Jeb and Jorge the Pontificator Ramos want me to speak Spanish?

Okay, I'll speak Spanish: *Enrique Peña Nieto es un FRAH-CAH-SAH-DOH!*

He's a *fracasado*—a failure!

When I'm president, I will *withdraw* our ambassador to Mexico!

I will do that to protest Enrique Peña Nieto's complicity in failing to be accountable for those missing students! I will do that to protest Enrique Peña Nieto's corrupt cronyism! I will do that to protest Enrique Peña Nieto's inability to keep El Chapo in prison!

Enrique Peña Nieto is a loser in the first category, and it is an outrage that this student-killer, this luxury-mansion thief, this Narco-enabler is even *allowed* to enter the United States!

I will be the best president Mexico has ever had without being elected president of Mexico!

I stand with the families of the 43 missing students!

And, at home, I will be the best president Latinos—LEGAL LATINOS—have ever had in the United States!

Yes, to the Hispanics—the *Silent Hispanic Majority*—that constitute 30 million law-abiding citizens of the United States! I speak for you and I have your interests at heart!

I have hired thousands and thousands of Latinos in my career, and they love me.

Why?

Because I am fair and honest and decent with them—and I respect them.

Do I need the Latino vote?

No, I can win without the Latino vote because, thanks to the Electoral College, white voters in the white states will cancel out Latinos' votes against me.

Do I want the Latino vote?

Of course! Because I'm going to be the best president for Latinos

144

ever. Bill Clinton didn't give Latinos immigration reform, and isn't Barack Obama derided as the Deporter-in-Chief who's done nothing, nothing, nothing for the delusional Dreamers?

The Silent Hispanic Majority understands full well how Barack Obama used them—twice. He promised them *everything* and delivered *nothing*.

No immigration reform. No hope for Dreamers. He didn't close down Guantánamo. He didn't do right by American citizens of Cuban origin whose assets were seized by a communist dictatorship. He didn't promote Hispanics in government.

By every measure, by every promise, Obama—and Bill Clinton before him—have used, abused, and screwed over Latinos.

Where, I ask again, was Nancy Pelosi, that racist piece of human shit, when Edgar Mora was being sacrificed on the altar of Terence Hallinan's political ambition?

Like a Judas, she betrayed the Latinos of San Francisco.

And so has Barack Obama!

And let me tell you that Hispanics are under attack—and I will put a stop to it.

Did you know?

Did you know that there is an ideological war being waged against Latinos in this country by political extremists?

The Climate of Hostility created by despicable anti-Latino bigots like Nancy Pelosi, Terence Hallinan, Gavin Newsom, and Lester Olmstead-Rose has repercussions around the country.

The same week! The same week! The same week that vandals desecrated the Carmel Mission where Junípero Serra is buried in California, vandals also attacked the Mexican Consulate in New York.

The Left hates Spain. The Right hates Mexico.

Did you know that?

Did you know that radical leftists hate everything that has to do with Spain and radical rightists hate everything that has to do with Mexico?

I love Spain! I love Mexico! I love the Spanish people! I love the Mexican people!

And I will defend Hispanics, Latinos, and Latin Americans like no other president has defended them!

Leftist losers attack the Spanish heritage of California and Rightist losers attack Mexican diplomats in New York!

These hate crimes are the direct result—what sociologists call "causal relation"—of the anti-Latino bigotry of the Democrats!

Those bigots that attack Junípero Serra don't know the truth; they rely on the lies Democrats feed them!

This is what Rubén Mendoza, an archaeology professor at the California State University, Monterey Bay, said of Saint Junípero Serra: "He constantly told his students in the seminary to commit themselves to indigenous people, commit themselves to the missionary enterprise for, quote, the salvation of humanity, and he truly embraced that as his calling. He came to these territories—California—convinced that he could save indigenous people."

And for that, this Spanish saint is attacked by anti-Hispanic hate criminals in California that exist only because of the Climate of Hostility created by racist pieces of human shit like Nancy Pelosi, Terence Hallinan, Gavin Newsom, and Lester Olmstead-Rose!

The attack on Junípero Serra is a measure of the hatred Democrats have for Hispanic culture and the contempt in which they hold the contributions of Spain to our country.

It's disgusting—and it ends when I'm in office.

And it gets worse!

Latinos are being encouraged to send another—an outrageous—racist piece of human shit to Washington, D.C.!

Did you know?

Did you know that Kamala Harris is running for the Senate?

Kamala Harris is a racist piece of human shit!

What I say is what I say!

And what I say is the truth!

A Latino voting for Kamala Harris is a masochist!

Did you know?

Did you know that when she was district attorney for San Francisco her D.A.'s office prosecuted Latinos to cover up the anti-Latino bias and bigotry in the San Francisco government?

Did you know? It's true!

Did you know that when she was district attorney for San Francisco, the San Francisco Human Rights Commission refused to provide services to Latinos?

It's true!

Virginia Harmon ran the Human Rights Commission, and she ordered that complaints filed by Latinos be disregarded. And Virginia Harmon is a renowned Sapphic racist piece of human shit who sought to deny Latino services! And—by the way—fat pig Virginia Harmon gives fat pig Rosie O'Donnell a run for her money when it comes to being a fat pig!

And is fat pig Virginia Harmon a racist piece of human shit that discriminates against Latinos?

Ask Edward Ilumin, who was ordered to refuse to investigate complaints filed by Latinos!

It's horrible, horrible, *horrible* the way San Francisco city government attacks Latinos!

And over at the District Attorney's Office, anti-Latino bigotry was the modus operandi when Kamala Harris was in charge.

Lisa Culbertson, who worked for Kamala Harris, targeted Latinos as part of a cover-up to prevent San Franciscans from knowing about the anti-Latino bigotry of city-funded agencies!

Makes sense! Makes racist sense!

Racist piece of human shit Lisa Culbertson was sucking up to racist piece of human shit Kamala Harris!

And now Kamala Harris, a racist piece of human shit, wants to be a United States senator?

Give *me* a break! Give *America* a break!

No more Democrat racist pieces of human shit who bamboozle Latinos!

147

Every Latino in California has to vote for Loretta Sánchez—*who is a Democrat, by the way, proof of my speaking up for the truth*—if Latinos are to make headway!

Where is Jorge Ramos?

Where is Jorge Ramos reporting on the anti-Latino bigotry that characterizes everything that Kamala Harris has done as district attorney in San Francisco and as attorney general of California?

Kamala Harris, that racist piece of human shit, cannot bring her anti-Latino bigotry to Washington, D.C.!

Where is Jorge Ramos on this?

Where is the immigration reform? Bill Clinton didn't deliver it in eight years in office. Barack Obama won't deliver it in his eight years in office.

Year after year, the Democratic bamboozles Latinos!

Empty promise after empty promise!

Remember 2006?

Remember the millions of Latinos across the country protesting for immigration reform?

Where is it?

Where is the immigration reform that the Democrats promised?

The Democrats lie to Latinos in the U.S. the way the PRI lies to Mexicans in Mexico!

A Latino who votes for the Democrats is like a Mexican who votes for the PRI: *a pobre pendejo!*

I promise you that I will be the best president for Latinos you can imagine—and I will do it without being married to a pre-Columbian relic!

A Latino who votes for a Democrat is like a Mexican who votes for the PRI: a masochist!

Make America Great Again!

Vote Trump.

14. We Let the Silent Majority Become the Noisy Majority

Our leaders are stupid!

We think we can bully the majority of the people in this country by hushing them up. That's what political correctness does—it silences dissent.

Now, I know I've had an exchange with Megyn Kelly, and I know I've called fat pig Rosie O'Donnell a fat pig—because, quite frankly, she is a fat pig.

And I did say a comment or two about Carly Fiorina, since she, like Sarah Jessica Parker, looks like a horse.

But horses are beautiful!

Remember Black Beauty?

Of course you do! Who doesn't remember Black Beauty?

I happen to think horse-face Carly Fiorina is a beautiful mare—I mean, woman.

And I know that these stupid, stupid opportunists have used this to label me a misogynist, or whatever.

But that's a misrepresentation of my position! That's a distortion of my free speech.

This country has used political correctness to stop people from speaking the truth.

Just because I say Rosie O'Donnell is a fat pig does not mean that she is *not* a fat pig.

Since when is the truth unacceptable?

Look, I believe in the words of Martin Luther King Jr., who said that you should judge a man or woman by the content of his or her character.

That's what I do.

But when you see something, think about it, and speak the truth—you're shamed.

Fat pig Rosie O'Donnell is a fat pig. That's the truth.

Can she be a good person and still be a fat pig? Probably.

But let's be honest, her own kid ran away—probably because she was trying to get away from that fat pig.

Can you imagine how many Oreos they are eating in that house?

I don't think there are enough Mexicans at Nabisco's new plant in Mexico—which, by the way, I will bring back to the U.S.—to make all the Oreos fat pig Rosie O'Donnell eats.

But when I say that, I'm accused of being antifeminist or antilesbian.

So, to silence my critics—the way they have *silenced* the Silent Majority—*but not for much longer*—I will quote from another woman, another lesbian, another liberal who agrees with me about the dangers of silencing the Silent Majority.

This is what Camille Paglia, who, by the way, is a very *handsome* dyke, has to say about Liberal Losers on American campuses bullying people into surrendering free speech.

"This is *madness!*" handsome lesbian Camille Paglia says. "The idea that somehow one cannot critique liberalism from the left, from the left wing of liberalism. I mean, *how* can people be so stupid? So, I'm this very powerful weapon, okay, being used *not* by the right against the left but rather by people who are *liberal* thinkers who have been enslaved by these poseurs, these racketeers, people who are pretending to be liberal but who are in fact just naive politically. I have been congratulated by women—people rush up to me at the end of my lectures—women of my age, women who are younger, who are *so sick* of being bullied by these sanctimonious *puritans* who call themselves feminists."

That's what she says.

America's Silent Majority is tired of being bullied by sanctimonious Leftist Losers into believing all this "politically correct" garbage.

I speak my mind and I speak the truth!

And I'm here to tell America—and the world—that the Silent

Majority is going to become the Noisy Majority!

The Silent Majority, believe me, is back, and I think we can use it somewhat differently. I don't think we have to call it a *silent* majority anymore, because they're not silent.

People are silent no longer.

They're disgusted with our incompetent politicians.

They're disgusted with the people who are giving our country away.

They're disgusted when they tell the border-patrol agents, who are good people and can do the job—they're disgusted when they allow people just to walk right in front of them, and they're standing there helpless, and people just pour into the country.

They're disgusted when a woman who is nine months pregnant walks across the border, has a baby, and you have to take care of that baby for the next 85 years.

They're disgusted by what's happening to our country. And you're going to look around. You're going to remember who the people are that are here, because we're doing something special.

This is a movement. We're going to make our country great again—believe me. We will make our country great again.

How can I be antifeminist when I support—and I am now endorsing—the views of one of the most important living social commentators this nation has produced?

She's so brilliant, I'm going to quote her again—on how Radical Feminists have infiltrated our school campuses to brainwash people and to bully people into capitulating to their one, specific brand of politically correct intolerance.

"A major failing of most feminist ideology is its dumb, ungenerous stereotyping of men as tyrants and abusers, when in fact—as I know full well, from my own mortifying lesbian experience—men are tormented by women's flirtatiousness and hemming and hawing, their manipulations and changeableness, their humiliating rejections," Camille Paglia says.

Does this sound like Megyn Kelly's treatment of me?

151

Yes, it does!

Does this sound like all those people with this mock outrage at my calling fat pig Rosie O'Donnell a fat pig?

Yes, it does!

She goes on, the brilliant Camille Paglia, speaking for the bullied and silent majority of Americans. She says: "If middle class feminists think they conduct their love lives perfectly rationally, without any instinctual influences from biology, they are imbeciles."

Feminists are imbeciles, Camille Paglia says.

Not me.

But I agree with her!

And so do the majority of the American people!

The Silent Majority.

Let me remind you that it was on November 3, 1969, when President Richard Nixon said, "And so tonight—to you, the great silent majority of my fellow Americans—I ask for your support."

And now, in 2015, my fellow Americans, I ask for your support as we move into the 2016 presidential election—months away!

I promise you that I will champion your right to be the Noisy Majority!

Can I hear some noise?

Can I hear some noise?

There!

America's Silent Majority is silent no more!

That's what I promise you if elected.

I promise you that I will let the majority of Americans—the majority of Americans who are tired of being bullied by the fascists of political correctness, by the bullies who want to impose amnesty for illegal aliens on us, by the know-it-alls who think that another government mess—Obamacare—is the right thing for America, and by the leeches who want to control how your hard-earned money is spent—rise up and speak out every day from the Oval Office.

Am I a populist?

Yes, I am, and I am a populist in the best tradition of populism in our country: *To speak for the common man from the highest office in the land!*

And part of what the Silent Majority wants to say is that we, as Americans—who, by the way, have come from every corner of the world—are a peace-loving people.

But we can only be at peace when we are strong.

Of the four wars in Ronald Reagan's lifetime, none came about because the U.S. was too strong!

And that strength is reflected in our willingness to reach out and speak to everyone, our friends, of course, but, more importantly, our adversaries.

Think Russia. Think Putin.

Listen, I'm very, very, very rich—I'm so rich, it's incredible.

And I am a billionaire because I know how to negotiate—trust me, the people I do business with are not nice, gentle people. They are mean, cutthroat, and vicious. That's why they're successful.

And the reason I'm successful is because I can negotiate with mean, cutthroat, vicious businessmen and businesswomen and reach deals that are good for everybody.

They make money. I make money—I make *a lot* of money—and everyone is happy.

That's how we have to approach Russia's Putin.

I would talk to him; I would get along with him.

Putin can be an asshole—just look at his complete military takeover of Syria—but I can also be an asshole!

And, believe me, in business, I've worked with hundreds and hundreds of world-class assholes.

I can be as big an asshole as anyone in the world!

And when I'm in the Oval Office, I will be the biggest asshole in the world if that's what it takes to protect America's interests.

Putin thinks he's an asshole?

Wait until he realizes that, unlike Obama, who was happy to pay the price of doing nothing in Syria rather than keeping his word, I'm prepared to go ballistic over taking care of the unfinished business—

the wreckage—Bush II and Obama have left in their wake!

I will be able to work with Putin because I'm a world-class negotiator when it comes to negotiating with world-class assholes. And I would make a deal with him.

Ronald Reagan sat down with Tip O'Neill, the most liberal guy in Congress. And they worked together because Ronald Reagan understood that you have to work with your adversaries if you want to get things done.

Listen, when we don't speak to people who are adversaries, terrible, terrible, terrible things happen.

Why didn't Bush II speak to Saddam Hussein?

He should have, and he would have come to the conclusion that there were no weapons of mass destruction in Iraq and that Iraq had nothing to do with September 11.

Instead, relying on fake information and fabricated intelligence, we went to war.

Give *me* a break! Give *America* a break!

And we are still paying for that war—and, quite frankly, we will continue to pay for that war for decades to come.

And Low-Energy Loser Jeb—who, by the way, wants to pretend to be the Eveready Energizer Bunny—believes that his brother kept us safe.

Well, that's not true.

Remember? Do you remember?

George W. Bush was given a classified review of the threats posed by Osama bin Laden on August 6, 2001. It was part of that morning's "presidential daily brief"—that's the top secret document prepared by America's intelligence agencies for the president's review every day before Bush II did whatever Dick "Darth Vader" Cheney told him to do. The report that morning was titled "Bin Laden Determined to Strike in U.S."

Hello?

How much more obvious does it have to be? Written in glow-in-the-dark crayons? Spelled out in cocaine lines for the Crackhead-in-

154

Chief?

You did know that, didn't you? You did know that George W. Bush was arrested for cocaine possession back in 1972? Yes, he was, like a pathetic drug addict who got away with it because he's white and his family is rich—and that sums up America's criminal justice system.

If you're rich and white, you get a pass.

And right now, we're giving Bush II another pass—when it comes to 9/11!

When you talk about George Bush, I mean, say what you want, the World Trade Center came down during his time. The World Trade Center came down during his reign. Blame him or not blame him, who cares?

The truth is that, less than a month after he was warned Osama bin Laden was poised to attack America "imminently," the World Trade Center was destroyed!

And then, Low-Energy Loser Jeb tweets, "How pathetic for @realdonaldtrump to criticize the president for 9/11. We were attacked & my brother kept us safe."

No, he didn't keep us safe.

Remember?

Remember Kurt Eichenwald writing in the *New York Times* on September 10, 2012?

I do!

Kurt Eichenwald—in the *New York Times*—reported: "The direct warnings to Mr. Bush about the possibility of a Qaeda attack began in the spring of 2001. By May 1, the Central Intelligence Agency told the White House of a report that 'a group presently in the United States' was planning a terrorist operation. Weeks later, on June 22, the daily brief reported that Qaeda strikes could be "imminent," although intelligence suggested the time frame was flexible."

Look it up!

The name of the article, you ask?

"The Deafness Before the Storm."

George W. Bush was *deaf* to the constant barrage of warnings about an imminent attack on American soil by Osama bin Laden!

They had already attacked the World Trade Center when they bombed the underground parking lot in 1993. Bill Clinton was president, but he was too busy sexually assaulting Monica Lewinsky to do anything about it. Obviously, screwing Monica Lewinsky and screwing her over were *his* priorities—not taking out Osama bin Laden when he had the chance to do so.

And, as the *New York Times* reported, and I quote, "In the aftermath of 9/11, Bush officials attempted to deflect criticism that they had ignored C.I.A. warnings by saying they had not been told when and where the attack would occur. That is true, as far as it goes, but it misses the point. Throughout that summer, there were events that might have exposed the plans, had the government been on high alert. Indeed, even as the Aug. 6 brief was being prepared, Mohamed al-Kahtani, a Saudi believed to have been assigned a role in the 9/11 attacks, was stopped at an airport in Orlando, Fla., by a suspicious customs agent and sent back overseas on Aug. 4. Two weeks later, another co-conspirator, Zacarias Moussaoui, was arrested on immigration charges in Minnesota after arousing suspicions at a flight school. But the dots were not connected, and Washington did not react."

I blame George W. Bush for ignoring the warnings and being deaf to the mounting evidence of an imminent attack being prepared by Osama bin Laden.

And when Low-Energy Loser Jeb claims that his brother kept us safe—oh, brother!

Is he full of shit or what?

Look, it's time that we Americans spoke the truth to ourselves.

That's the only way we're going to move forward, by speaking the truth. And the truth is that I don't blame anybody for 9/11, but it's possible that something could have been done that was obviously better than the worst attack ever perpetrated on the United States.

What do I mean?

Well, to start with, under Bush II we had a very weak immigration system. If we had had the immigration laws I'm proposing, none of the hijackers would have been able to enter the country. We also know that under Bush II, the FBI, CIA, and National Security Council weren't sharing information with each other. If I'm president, I want to have my three most important agencies communicating to each other and coordinating with each other. And, of course, I want *honesty*. George Tenet, who ran the CIA under Bush II, admits that he knew in advance that there was going to be an attack, but wasn't honest about it and didn't speak up.

We need leaders who are honest and blunt, leaders who are not intimidated by political correctness and who do not mince words.

That's how we've gotten ourselves into this mess. And I don't mince words: Clinton could have taken out Osama bin Laden, but didn't. Bush II could have taken the threat Osama bin Laden presented to our homeland seriously, but didn't.

And our reaction to 9/11—beginning with the invasion of Iraq in 2003—has been terrible, terrible, terrible.

Do you know why I have my own plane?

Yes, it's because I'm rich—I'm really, really rich! But I have my own plane because I refuse to be frisked by the TSA!

I refuse to be humiliated and take off my shoes at the airport—and I don't think that my fellow Americans should be subjected to this bullshit "feel-good" so-called "security" that is meaningless.

Americans are now living like cowards!

Did you know they closed down Wall Street? Have you been there? There are barricades, cameras, SWAT teams, dogs! It's the way fugitives or cowards live.

We live like cowards! We really do! And we live like cowards because we are no longer the home of the free and land of the brave.

We are the home of the chicken and the land of cowards.

And you can blame our reaction to 9/11 for that.

The truth is that the World Trade Center was destroyed under George W. Bush's watch. And the more painful truth is that more

Americans have died *after* September 11 than *on* September 11.

And these Americans have died in a needless, stupid, terrible war of invasion!

Low-Energy Loser Jeb doesn't get it. Low-Energy Loser Jeb doesn't understand that we are not going to let him and his family rewrite history!

When Jeb says his brother kept us safe, he means his brother kept us complacent! I'm here to tell you that safety is not complacency. Low-Energy Loser Jeb believes the Bushes can rewrite history to get him into the White House.

That's not surprising. I mean, you could shove an Eveready battery up his ass, press it against his prostate, and Low-Energy Jeb would still be Low-Energy.

That's how pathetic he is.

And he's a pathetic liar.

Low-Energy Loser Jeb wants America to forget the thousands and thousands of American casualties in a terrible, terrible, terrible war.

You want proof?

How about the word of a Marine who fought in Iraq?

Last year, in 2014, Falluja fell to Al Qaeda. Back in 2004, Adam Banotai was a 21-year-old sergeant and squad leader in the Marine Corps when we invaded Falluja. His unit seized control of the government early in the campaign—which, by the way, resulted in his men suffering seven shrapnel and bullet injuries the first day.

During that heroic 2004 invasion of Falluja, a restive, insurgent-held city in Iraq, he and his fellow Marines liberated that city. His unit seized control of the government center early in the campaign.

Ten years later, Sunni insurgents, all part of Al Qaeda, gained control of the city that Americans fought so hard to liberate.

Do you know what he said?

I do!

I have it right here!

Adam Banotai told reporters this: "I don't think anyone had the grand illusion that Falluja or Ramadi was going to turn into Disneyland, but none of us thought it was going to fall back to a jihadist insurgency. It made me sick to my stomach to have that thrown in our face, everything we fought for so blatantly taken away."

The Iraq War has made us all sick to our stomachs as Americans—and impoverished us as a nation.

That's how we have squandered our wealth! That's how we have asked so many to sacrifice so much. That's how so many Americans have paid the ultimate price—for a war that was a mistake, for a cause that is lost.

And Low-Energy Loser Jeb thinks America wants another Bush in the White House!

The terrible, terrible, terrible truth is that Dick Cheney and George W. Bush—and their administration—gave us Barack Obama, because it was such a disaster those last three months that Abraham Lincoln couldn't have been elected!

I know that. You know that. Everyone knows that.

And do you know what?

I can't apologize for the truth.

And as a result, we've had Obama, who is a terrible, terrible president who has accomplished nothing but shoving Obamacare down the throats of the American people and given us terrible, terrible deals—Iran, the Pacific Rim countries, you name it!

How did this happen?

I know how it happened.

This has happened because the Silent Majority has not spoken up!

The Silent Majority has been bullied.

Listen to smart, handsome lesbians! Listen to Camille Paglia when she says, and I quote her here, "When the media get locked in their Northeastern ghetto and become slaves of the feminist establishment and fanatical special interests, the American audience ends up looking to conservative voices for common sense. As a libertarian Democrat, I protest against this self-defeating tyranny of political correctness."

That's what this is, what the media has become: *A champion of the tyranny of political correctness that bullies the Silent Majority into submission. . . .*

You don't have to be a muffin diver to get it!

And this stops!

The Silent Majority is back, and we're going to take our country back.

We are going to rise up and speak and let our voices be heard!

We need high energy!

We need a high-energy president.

That's why Ben Carson can't be president.

I know Ben Carson. He's a good man. He's a great American.

But he's low energy.

Watching Ben Carson is like watching rice simmer, Uncle Ben's rice.

We already have a black president with such low energy he might as well be comatose. In fact, the only time Barack Obama has any energy is when he's about to shoot a selfie with Beyoncé. That says more about Michelle Obama than anything else!

But Uncle Ben Carson?

If we had Uncle Ben as president, it would be like having Calvin Coolidge back in the White House! We'd need to take his pulse to make sure he was still alive!

Uncle Ben Carson is low, low energy!

And I say this as a compassionate American who wants the best for America!

My critics don't understand the breadth of Americans' compassion, acceptance, and respect for individual freedom.

They would have you believe that I'm a misogynist. That I'm antifeminist. That I'm hostile to members of minorities—whether they're Muslim or members of the LGBTQ community.

But they're wrong.

Which of my critics would believe that I am standing here, making this declaration on behalf of the Silent Majority, by invoking a lesbian feminist?

Which of my critics would believe that Camille Paglia and I stand shoulder to shoulder on so many issues?

Would a misogynist do that? Would someone who doesn't respect women—and their abilities and intellects—do that?

As your president I will continue to surprise the bigoted, narrow-minded Thought Police of the Liberal Elite that is everywhere on our college campuses and in the media.

Remember, it was Richard Nixon who flew to Beijing to make peace with China!

Remember, it was Ronald Reagan who made peace with Soviet Union—and he was responsible for the Berlin Wall coming down!

And it will be President Trump who allows America's Silent Majority to be heard!

I want to be the voice of the Silent Majority! I want to let those who have been bullied into submission by the fascism of political correctness be liberated!

Let's be perfectly clear about this: political correctness creates a climate of hostility against modernity!

Day 1 in office, this ends!

Day 1 in office, the Silent Majority will be heard!

Day 1 in office, the tyranny of political correctness ends in Washington!

I want the Silent Majority to become the Noisy Majority!

Make America Great Again!

Vote Trump.

15. Why the Media Is Not Trusted

Our leaders are stupid!

They think they have to respect the media.

Quite frankly, the media today—by which I mean the bulk of reporters working today—deserve no respect.

For the most part, you can't respect people in general because most people aren't worthy of respect. That's especially true of people in the media.

I've said that we are led by stupid, stupid people—very, very stupid people—and I mean it.

And part of the reason we are led by very stupid, stupid people is because we have even more stupid, stupid reporters misinforming the American public!

When I'm falsely accused of race-baiting or engaging in White Identity politics or wearing a hairpiece, the sheer stupidity of such claims is so great that no one with a brain can take them seriously.

And yet, I see hours and hours of talking heads and pundits going over this or that as if such ridiculous things had any merit.

Race-baiting?

White Identity politics?

A hairpiece?

Give *me* a break! Give *America* a break!

And I blame the media. Instead of reporting the truth, the media go along with the lies.

I mean, look at the Middle East.

If you were to believe the media, you'd think that Saudi Arabia was our ally.

Yes, we buy oil from them. Yes, we sell military weapons to them.

But Saudi Arabia is not our ally.

I saw a report yesterday. There's so much oil, all over the world, they don't know where to dump it. And Saudi Arabia says, "Oh, there's too much oil." They came back yesterday. Did you see the report? They want to *reduce* oil production.

Do you think they're our friends? They're not our friends.

And they *can't* be our friends—ever.

Why?

It's simple.

America, a democracy comprised of free men, women, and intersex persons, cannot be friends with a country where women are denied their fundamental human rights.

In Saudi Arabia, women are not given driver's licenses. In Saudi Arabia, women cannot marry whom they love. In Saudi Arabia, women do not have reproductive rights. In Saudi Arabia, gays and lesbians are executed.

In Saudi Arabia, it's forbidden to eat bacon. In Saudi Arabia, you can't order a gin and tonic.

Ban bacon? No cocktails?

These people are savages—and we cannot have them as friends. These are backward desert dwellers that just happen to be sitting on an ocean of oil. That's all.

That's all that they are—*strategic* partners.

But nothing more!

Why?

Because they are not our friends because American cannot be friends with a nation that oppresses its own people and is beholden to beliefs best left to the Middle Ages!

But the media don't speak honestly about what's going on.

And this is the case about everything!

Take Bill Clinton and Monica Lewinsky.

Where was the press when this story broke?

Oh, sure, the story was covered from many, many angles—but not, perhaps, the most important one: Monica Lewinsky is a Latina.

Did you know that?

Did you know that Monica Lewinsky is a first-generation

American, the daughter of an immigrant from San Salvador?

Granted, she's not a Ten like Jennifer López, but Monica Lewinsky is as much a Latina as Jennifer López!

I think that, when the scandal broke, the media were derelict in their moral obligation to report to the American people that what Bill Clinton did to that woman, Ms. Lewinsky, was an act of Imperialism, another chapter in the sad narrative of an Anglo male sexually assaulting a Latina woman.

Where was the National Association of Hispanic Journalists when this story came out?

Where was Jorge Ramos to report on this?

Everyone knows what the Lewinskys are a well-known Salvadoran Jewish family. Those Latino Losers can't be that fucking stupid!

Where were all the Hispanic, Latino, and Latin advocacy groups?

They were absent. All of them were missing in action! Or inaction, since they don't care about covering anything that is critical of Democrats.

Not even when Barack Obama became the Deporter-in-Chief!

Why were they absent?

I know why.

Because they're *assholes*. You know, some of the media are among the worst people I've ever met. I mean, a really good percentage is really a terrible group of people. They're assholes.

They're stupid. They're incompetent. They lie. They can't write a grocery list. They are not just jealous, but they are outright envious of successful people.

They will eat any crap you put out as a spread during a news conference, they're that petty and desperate for anything that's free, even stale doughnuts.

It's disgusting.

Have you seen the disgusting spreads they put in their green rooms?

No wonder they can't think straight, with so much sugar and preservatives in their bodies.

No wonder Charlie Rose looks like a walking mummy. No wonder Gayle King looks like she wants to give Rosie O'Donnell a run for her money in the fat pig category.

Why can't Gayle King interview Hillary Clinton?

Because there's no camera lens wide enough to get both their sets of wide hips in the same frame!

I mean, it was only after I saw what CNN puts out for their guests in the green room that I thought, "Shit, if I had to subsist on this garbage, well, who can blame Don Lemon for sucking white cock just to get the taste of that crap out of his mouth?"

Who does Don Lemon think he is? Does he think anybody ever thought he was straight?

Coming out of the closet for him was like Richard Simmons coming out of the closet: superfluous!

Don Lemon, give me a break!

Do you know that African Americans have no respect for him? They don't!

Blacks ridicule Don Lemon as a modern-day Uncle Tom.

It's true!

This doesn't surprise me, since—by the way—Don Lemon is a black man who sucks white cock.

He's no different from Anderson Cooper.

If you don't live in New York, you probably don't know that across from the Time Warner Center on Columbus Circle—where, by the way, the Trump International Hotel is located—is also Central Park South.

So, on Central Park South is the New York Health & Racquet Club.

Anderson Cooper works out there—and do you know what?

When Anderson Cooper is in the locker room, he showers with a towel wrapped around his waist.

He says he's afraid that, with cell phones being everywhere

these days, someone might shoot a picture of his privates and sell it to a tabloid.

Can you believe it?

Can you believe it?

Anderson Cooper doesn't want the world to know that his left testicle hangs lower than his right?

Give *me* a break! Give *America* a break!

Don't you see?

Hiding the truth and betraying the public's trust, these are the professional "skills" of the losers at CNN.

Stupid is as stupid does.

Stupid is as stupid reports.

CNN is stupid any way you look at it.

How stupid is CNN?

Do you know that, according to the CNN, I'm like blue jeans? It's true.

Blue jeans go with everything! And CNN had Breaking News saying that I complement everyone.

Complement, with an *e*, not an *i*.

What I *said* was that I give compliments to everyone. And CNN *reported* that I *complement* everyone—meaning, I think, that I am a perfect match for everyone.

I'm Everyman!

Stupid is as stupid does.

Stupid is as stupid reports.

Do you see how stupid, stupid, stupid the media are? CNN has retards working for them who flunked English grammar back in junior high!

If they are too stupid to know the difference between *giving* a compliment and *being* a complement, what can we expect?

Stupid is as stupid publishes.

That means Arianna Huffington.

What can I say about Arianna Huffington? I could say she's stupid, but I won't say she's stupid even if I think she's stupid.

Even if I think she looks like a stray dog and is a stupid woman.

What I *will* say is that Arianna Huffington—and Huffington isn't her real name, by the way, because she's an immigrant from that mess of a country, Greece.

Why the European Union hasn't expelled Greece from the eurozone, I don't know. Why *we* haven't expelled Arianna Huffington from the United States, I don't know either!

Let's be honest. Ariana Huffington has terrible, terrible, terrible judgment.

Just one example!

Arianna Huffington married a homosexual.

Did you know that?

Did you know that she married a gay guy and didn't have enough common sense to realize she was marrying a gay guy?

Hello, Arianna?

Didn't that DVD *Adam Does San Francisco* give you a clue? Didn't your husband having sex with men in the guest bedroom give you a hint?

How stupid do you have to be not to realize you married a cocksucker?

I'll tell you how stupid you have to be: You have to be Liza Minnelli stupid, that's how stupid.

Give *me* a break! Give *America* a break!

And her lack of common sense, her bad judgment, and her self-serving self-denials are evident in how she—and the rest of the putrid media—cover issues.

Where are, for instance, the media to be found challenging by what right Hillary Clinton is running for office?

It's hard to believe she's even running for president. You wouldn't believe it was possible after what she's done, with her emails and the email server. What she did is totally illegal.

That server, the lies about the emails, the mishandling of classified information, ordering the server company to erase memory, and her subterfuge are all criminal, absolutely criminal.

167

The whole thing is terrible for our country. The whole thing is Watergate on steroids. Really, it is.

I mean, Hillary Hippo Hips Hypocrite claims—claims—and I say *claims* with hesitation because, quite frankly, I don't believe her bullshit claims.

But she *claims* that she wanted total privacy, for whatever reason. The truth is she would have had more privacy had she used a government email account!

Why aren't the media talking about the sense of entitlement of this pathetic, arrogant autocrat who thinks the rules don't apply to her, because the Clintons—like the Bushes—are above the rule of law?

Hey, CNN, give *America* a break!

And give America professional reporting!

"TRUMP: MY HAIR IS NOT THAT BAD!"

"TRUMP: I COMPLEMENT EVERYONE!"

Unbelievable!

Stupid is as stupid does.

Stupid is as stupid reports.

Why can't more reporters be like Matt Drudge—thorough, fair, and accurate? I really, really respect that guy.

But most of the rest of the media?

Asshole is as asshole reports or broadcasts!

I can tell you most of America believes that one of the biggest media assholes today is *Forbes* magazine.

What's wrong with those losers?

Are they jealous—or just stupid?

I'm running for president, and *Forbes* reports my wealth at $4.5 billion? That's nuts! They have no credibility!

I'm worth much, much more than what *Forbes* says. You know, I don't look good, to be honest. I look better if I'm worth $10 billion than if I'm worth $4.5 billion. I think *Forbes* is trying to make me as poor as possible.

See?

The media work to make me look bad!

And the ones who look bad are the assholes at *Forbes* magazine! All I can say is that *Forbes* is a bankrupt magazine and doesn't know what they are talking about. It's embarrassing to me.

That's the truth about how America feels about the media: *embarrassment!*

And the truth is that the incompetence of the media is what's boosting my support.

It's true!

My supporters see in me someone who is a truth-speaker, and I say out loud what they are thinking!

Bush II lied to us, and it was a mistake to invade Iraq.

Obama has been a complete disaster, so terrible that even the Nobel Peace Prize committee wants the Peace Prize back.

The world is a more dangerous place, with ISIS beheading people, Christians being crucified, China's economic might threatening global financial stability, Russia taking over the wreckage we left behind in the Middle East, our uncontrolled borders producing an invasion of illegal immigration, and corporate America betraying the American worker by shipping jobs overseas.

We are not respected and we are threatened.

And the media—with buffoons on the air—contribute to the crisis.

Every word that comes out of Brian Williams's mouth is a lie, including "and" and "the."

Every word that Maureen Dowd writes is cynicism.

Every Breaking News that Wolf Blitzer announces is a nonevent.

Is it any wonder that the American public has no faith in journalists? Is it any wonder Americans are tired of the personality-driven drivel?

Everyone knew you were gay, Don Lemon, so there was no need to come out! And everyone knows your left testicle hangs lower than your right, Anderson Cooper, so there's no need to be paranoid with the towels in the locker room!

169

Everyone knows that Jorge Ramos will *never* be an American until he hires — the fucking cheapskate — a voice coach.

And, of course, the *New Yorker* magazine will never be able to tell the difference between a cactus and a tuber!

I'll admit it. I've probably been a little childish. But you know what? This is a campaign. If you look at what I've said, I've always been *responding* to attacks. I'm a counterpuncher.

Marco Rubio, that little boy, is a liar!

Oh, excuse me!

Men lie. Little boys fib!

And Marco Rubio *fibbed* about his parents. They weren't immigrants who came to find a better life; they were political refugees fleeing Castro after Castro screwed them over.

Let's be clear!

The Rubios emigrated to the United States in 1956 because they opposed Fulgencio Batista. Then, Fidel Castro won! And they went back!

Can you believe it!

They! Went! Back!

Why?

Because the Rubio family *supported* Fidel Castro — they were *Fidelistas*.

And then, after the Revolution begins to devour its own, the Rubios run back to the U.S. — not as emigrants, but as political refugees.

See?

Little *boy* Marco Rubio *fibbed*, and the press gives him a free pass.

But the media shouldn't give him a free pass. There's no shame in being the son of Commie-loving losers, is there?

But I want to ask: Is America ready for the son-of-*Fidelistas* to sit in the Oval Office?

And, more importantly, is America ready for Marco Rubio, who first runs away from his family's pro-*Castro* past?

He's not a real man who can take it like a man, but a little boy whose feelings have to be spared.

Do you want me to speak Spanish?

Marco Rubio is a little boy—*un nene, un llorón,* or as they say in Little Havana, *una marica.*

Sometimes, part of making a deal is denigrating your competition. And I have had to be combative with the press to get my message out to the American people.

I can't count on moronic editors and asinine reporters. I have to push through the incompetence of the media, even if I have to be in-your-face confrontational—which, by the way, is not my nature since I'm, at the end of the day, a shy and modest man, humble and solicitous.

But not during a news conference!

Just ask former wetback Jorge Ramos!

And if you can't take it, then you shouldn't be in the game.

That's why America believes I'll be a great president. That's why America believes that I will be successful in looking out for our nation.

In an age filled with *trash* like the Kardashians and *freaks* like Caitlyn Jenner as part of the wallpaper of our lives—no offense to your family, Kanye West, since there's nothing wrong with your family that a simple divorce won't cure—America longs for a truth-speaker!

And I will continue to speak the truth!

And the truth is that with me in the Oval Office, America will have so many victories that at some point, they're going to be coming out of your ears!

Have to be careful! Nose, ears, eyes. Those are the only places I'm talking about!

And, personally, one of the greatest disappointments I continue to encounter is the inability of the press to understand my vision.

One of the greats who believed in broad strokes was Ronald Reagan, but the media do not report this. Of course I'm detailed-oriented, very detail-oriented, in fact, since that's what it takes to make billion-dollar deals that are successful.

But I am a person who does not necessarily believe in plans that have 14 steps. Because when the second step gets out of whack, you're screwed. I don't think the voters care about specifics. I think the press cares, but I've never had a voter ask for my policy papers.

That doesn't mean that, sensitive to the media, I'm not offering policy statements—which are being rolled out over the course of the campaign.

But the media are only interested in these position papers to get bogged down in the details while forgetting the broad vision that is necessary to make America great again.

And that's sad.

When the only trusted journalists are satirists, then that speaks to the moral depravity of American journalism today.

I know because I have read—and continue to read—so many articles filled with lies about me.

I understand marketing, but it's one thing to work an angle to sell newspapers, magazines, or get more viewers, but it's another thing to lie outright.

American journalism is filled with idiots and liars—and that's a tragedy.

But that's why millions and millions of angry Americans support me! They have had it with the lies of these idiots and liars!

Remember the CBNC debate?

What a bunch of lying losers!

The three moderators were losers!

Carlos Quintanilla is a Hispanic. You do know that, right? And in the words of Abraham Lincoln, Hispanics "are most decidedly a race of mongrels." That's what Abraham Lincoln said of the Mexicans, not me!

And that's how Carlos Quintanilla conducted himself at the debate. He was a half-breed, mongrel retard displaying the vices of the white man and the savagery of the Indian with a feather.

The others—Caucasians—were also losers.

172

John Harwood, as we all know, is a comic book version of a journalist and lacks *cojones*. He is the kind of eunuch that explains the demise of the straight while male in American society. He really has no balls and he really represents why America loses at everything. He's a pathetic loser.

What can be said of Becky Quick? She's not a fat pig, but she wasn't very quick, was she? I think the dictionary people at Oxford are going to Photoshop her picture next to the word *bimbo* in the 2016 edition. I'm not surprised.

Are you? Becky-Not-Very-Quick is a stupid, stupid, bimbo!

CNBC will never be a winner if they market their brand with these three pathetic losers.

I know. I know about marketing and building brands. My success is all about marketing.

Marketing, I get. I call it truthful hyperbole. It's an innocent form of exaggeration—and a very effective form of promotion.

When I read an article that has a brazen lie, I stop reading the story and toss it aside.

I say what most Americans believe. That's why voters have great confidence in me. It's because I really have been successful in business—and in life.

As Walter Cronkite used to say, "That's the way it is!"

Make America Great Again!

Vote Trump.

16. Defending America as a Brand

Our leaders are stupid!

Our leaders do not understand that America is more than a place; it is a hope.

And however odd it may seem, America is also a *brand*.

That may sound crass, but that's the truth: America is a brand, the most important brand on earth.

That brand has been ruined by Bush II and Obama.

No one respects us!

Do you think illiterate peasants sneaking across the border respect us? Do you think Putin, moving into Syria, respects us?

Give *me* a break! Give *America* a break!

America, the brand, is in tatters.

So how do we fix it? How does the Trump administration go about turning things around?

History shows the way.

Did you know that the Statue of Liberty was successfully *rebranded*?

It was!

I live in New York, and New York is filled with iconic buildings and monuments that are recognized the world over. I happen to own some of the most important—and iconic—properties in New York.

But one of the monuments that is known the world over is, of course, the Statue of Liberty.

Lady Liberty stands in New York Harbor, a beacon of hope to the world.

Do you know the true story of the Statue of Liberty?

You know it's a gift from French schoolchildren, of course. But that's only the beginning. That's only one detail—and a small detail—about the Statue of Liberty.

So here's the story.

The Statue of Liberty was a gift from France to the people of the United States to commemorate the end of the Civil War—and the North's victory over the South.

Did you know that? Did you know that the Statue of Liberty is a Civil War monument?

Take a look at the Statue of Liberty.

Ever look at her feet? If you have, you've noticed the slave's broken shackles—freedom and liberation! This is the liberty the Statue of Liberty proclaims to all—freedom from human bondage.

So, the French, being French, gave this gift to America.

And America, being gracious, accepted the gift.

It didn't occur to Americans that, perhaps, this gift was an affront.

I mean, how would the French feel if America built a giant guillotine as big as the Eiffel Tower and shipped it off to Paris?

Would the French want a giant guillotine to compete with the skyline, a constant, horrific reminder of the excesses of the Reign of Terror?

Of course not!

And, not surprising, Americans got tired of the idea of having this huge, humongous, enormous Civil War monument in New York Harbor.

No one wants to be reminded that the U.S.—*alone in the New World*—had a civil war to end slavery!

Did you know that?

Did you know that the savages in Mexico abolished slavery without resorting to a civil war? Did you know that the even more savage Brazilians also put an end to slavery without a civil war?

It's embarrassing, I know, but most Americans—and certainly New Yorkers—were not too keen on this giant Civil War monument reminding us of our own savagery!

The Statue of Liberty had to be taken down—or rebranded.

It's true!

We had to *repurpose* and *rebrand* the Statue of Liberty.

175

The solution was simple. It turned out that the Statue of Liberty was located next to Ellis Island, where immigrants were arriving.

You know why immigrants arrived at Ellis Island and not New York itself, don't you?

It was because these disgusting, impoverished peasants had to be disinfected and deloused before they were allowed to enter New York City!

These shiploads of immigrants, full of germs, were destitute, illiterate, and had to be checked out to make sure they weren't sick. Many were denied entry, and were sent back.

Did you know that?

It was this coincidence—millions coming to America and arriving on an island near the largest Civil War monument in the nation—that gave rise for an opportunity to rebrand the Statue of Liberty.

Emma Lazarus, a poet, was asked to come up with something to help rebrand the Statue of Liberty. She wrote "The New Colossus"— with these immortal lines: "Give me your tired, your poor,/Your huddled masses yearning to breathe free."

Brilliant!

The Statue of Liberty would no longer represent the failure of the United States to end slavery without resorting to a protracted civil war, but it would be a beacon of hope to the world's—*let's face it*—peasants.

Tired. Poor. Huddled masses.

And germ-filled.

I can tell you that this doesn't describe the people living in Trump Tower on Fifth Avenue!

No matter!

I'll bet anything you didn't know that the Statue of Liberty was the largest *Civil War monument* in the nation!

See? Rebranding was a success!

Well, after the fiasco of Bush II and Obama, America has to be rebranded!

I'm serious! Some people still don't get it. They don't think this election is about turning this country around.

Do you know what Salma Hayek, the Mexican actress married to a French billionaire, for whom—by the way—I have a great deal of respect, simply because she's a Ten, said?

She said, "This is not a reality show. America is not a reality show. This is not a popularity contest. This is not Miss America or Miss Universe."

She's right.

This is not a reality show!

But this is an election to restore America's greatness!

We have work to do! We have much to repair!

After the Reign of Darth Vader—Dick Cheney—and the disastrous misadventures of the Obama-Clinton foreign policy, the world expects us to atone for what we've done wrong.

For instance, did you know that, for a time, the U.S. was classified by our friends, like Canada, as a nation that practiced torture?

You can thank Dick Cheney and his waterboarding—which did nothing but give us bullshit confessions and nonsensical information by desperate men who invented things to say so as to stop the torture.

Did you know that Canada, for a brief time, was giving *political asylum* to Americans—since the U.S., according to the Canadian government, practiced torture and Canada grants asylum to "refugees" from countries fleeing a country that practices torture?

Unbelievable!

But that's the kind of depravity that took place during Bush II.

And with Obama, things are not much better!

Under the Kenyan Socialist—and his pathetic sidekick, Hillary Hippo Hips Hypocrite—we are a nation that protects child molesters, child rapists, and pedophiles!

Under the Obama-Clinton regime, we are a criminal nation that refuses to give accused men their day in court!

177

Unbelievable!

That's not who we are as a people or who we are as a nation—denying the men in Guantánamo a day in court!

Unbelievable!

And once we rebrand America, we will be able to move forward and make America into a nation of winners once again.

How do we atone?

Listen to this, Salma Hayek!

When Jimmy Carter was president, he negotiated a deal to hand over the Panama Canal to Panama.

Everyone thought he was nuts!

I thought he was nuts!

Give the Panama Canal to the Panamanians?

That was a recipe for disaster—that's what I thought, along with almost every Republican in the country.

But it went through—and I'm man enough to admit I was mistaken.

Panama has managed the Panama Canal for decades in an exemplary manner. No complaints.

Do you see?

There are times when doing the right thing turns out to be the right business decision, too.

Now, for decades, Cuba has demanded that the U.S. return the Guantánamo Naval Base to Cuba.

I'm prepared to state now that I believe in bold moves that will help restore American leadership in the world. There are times when, like Jimmy Carter, we can signal strength through confidence.

I'm prepared to hand over Guantánamo Naval Base to Cuba—and lift the embargo—on one condition: free elections in Cuba.

If Raúl Castro allows free elections, the United States, once the United Nations certifies the election results, will hand over Guantánamo Naval Base and lift the U.S. embargo within 24 hours.

It's that simple.

The U.S. may have needed the Guantánamo Naval Base back in

1903, but with today's technology, we don't need it. And if there are free and fair elections held in Cuba, the purpose for the trade embargo ceases to exist!

To be a great dealmaker, you have to be flexible. I'm prepared to make a deal with that closet-case, Raúl Castro.

Why?

Because there's no great dealmaker I've ever seen who's rigid. You have to go with the punches a little bit. And if you don't it's going to be a long day on Sunday.

So, Raúl, you want Guantánamo back and the embargo lifted? Guess what?

I want free elections in Cuba.

You give me what I want—and you get what you want.

And making this deal will be terrific for *America the Brand* throughout Latin America!

In business, sometimes doing the right thing is also doing the profitable thing!

That's what's made me billions: crafting deals that make each party better off!

Cuba gets that antiquated naval base—which, by the way, was transformed into a torture chamber in violation of the Geneva Convention by Bush II and then Obama went along for the ride since practicing torture is how African presidents run their countries!

Obama. Kenya. Hello?

Guantánamo. Torture. Hello?

This is what happens when you have a narcissist man-child in the Oval Office!

Bush II's stupidity + Obama's narcissism = the erosion of America the Beautiful and America the Brand.

And taking care of a brand is a difficult thing.

Not everyone can do it.

Take, for example, Susan Sarandon.

Forty years ago she established her brand when she played Janet in *The Rocky Horror Picture Show*. When that film—can you believe it's been four decades already?—was first released, Susan Sarandon, with her perky breasts and lovely smile, was easily a high Eight!

It's true! She was a high Eight, almost bordering on a low Nine! But now?

Have you seen her? Have you seen her recently?

She's raising money for this charity or that charity. I saw her raising money for Heifer International.

Well, Susan, you're now a Three.

And you're a Three because you've let yourself go! You look like an old cow, an old heifer!

Really, you do!

Of course Hillary Hippo Hips Hypocrite has hips so wide she looks like she gave birth to a herd of cattle, but Susan Sarandon?

A heifer is a cow that hasn't produced a calf. Susan Sarandon certainly knows how to pick charities to support with unintended irony!

I mean, isn't that a conflict of interest? By supporting heifers, isn't Susan Sarandon, in a way, supporting herself?

What happened?

I'll tell you what happened!

She gave up on her brand!

She got fame. She got money. She got a man.

Who could ask for anything more?

How about asking you to defend your brand?

She doesn't care. The same way that Obama doesn't care about America's brand, Susan doesn't care about her personal brand.

Well, Susan, why are you a groupie of the *Hillary Horror Campaign Show*? Why are you rooting for that pathetic loser—she was *against* gay marriage until she was for it, she was *against* gays and lesbians serving in the military before she was for it, she was *against* arresting child rapists raping children under U.S. military protection until she was for arresting pedophiles—when you could really redeem your brand by aligning yourself with the Silent Majority?

180

May I remind you, my audience—and Susan—about the *Rocky Horror Picture Show?* May I remind you why generations of American youth—even the slacker Millennials—flock to it?

It's just a jump to the left!

You know that.

And then?

It's just a jump to the right!

You know that, too.

And what does Trump offer?

A pelvic thrust that really will drive the world insane!

Well, it's time for America to drive the world insane!

Jump to the right, America! And then we'll give the world a pelvic thrust!

It's time for the world to go insane with joy at the sight of a resurgent America!

America the Beautiful must be America the Powerful!

That's our brand.

What's destroyed our credibility in the world—which, by the way, is integral to our branding as a superpower—is our failed foreign policy.

May I remind you?

The Barack Obama–Hillary Clinton policy in Syria collapsed completely!

There is no way in the world that America's foreign policy was to hand over Syria to the Russians so the Russians could establish a stronghold in the Middle East.

But that's what happened.

And when the Russians began their occupation of Syria, best friends Barack and Hillary went their separate ways, betraying the lack of principles—and *planning*—of the incompetent misrule by this administration!

Hillary Hippo Hips Hypocrite called for a robust approach to Syria, including establishing a no-fly zone. Barack "Nobel Peace Prize Winner of Endless Wars" Obama called for the status quo:

181

allowing the Russians to solidify their presence in Syria while the U.S. retreated!

We are led by very stupid, stupid people who don't understand how to protect us.

The schism between Obama and Clinton diminishes America's brand.

Unbelievable!

We are in this predicament because we are seen as weak.

Do you think that if Putin thought we were strong he would have annexed Crimea?

Of course not!

Do you think that if Putin thought we were strong he would have muscled into Syria?

Of course not!

Do you think if Putin thought we were strong he would have negotiated a secret deal behind our back with Iraq, Syria, and Iran?

Of course not!

And what Russia is doing, *everybody else is also doing*, from the Chinese who steal our secrets and launch cyberattacks, to the Mexicans who steal our jobs and flood our cities with drugs!

I want to have a military that's so strong, so powerful, so modern, has the greatest equipment in the world, that everybody says, "We're not gonna mess with them."

We don't have that now!

And that's because our brand is in tatters — and no one respects us.

You know, I'm on a lot of covers, I think more than almost any supermodel, but in a way that's a sign of respect.

People are respecting what you're doing.

I want the world to react to what we're doing — and not in a bad way.

Bombing Doctors Without Borders in Afghanistan?

That's crazy!

That destroys a brand the way James William Lewis almost

destroyed Tylenol when he tampered with the capsules and laced them with potassium cyanide. It took Tylenol years to rebuild its brand after the 1982 murders.

It will also take us years—and decisive action—to restore America the Brand.

What do we expect?

After Bush II destroyed Iraq. After Bush II engaged in torture so brazenly that, for a while, Canada was granting asylum to Americans. After Obama gave the world ISIS. After Obama allowed the Russians to take over Syria. After Obama allowed child molesters to abuse more children than Perv Catholic priests. After Obama bombed a humanitarian hospital.

And Doctors Without Borders, the recipient of a Nobel Peace Prize, accused Barack Obama of a *war crime!*

Nobel Peace Prize–winner Barack Obama is accused of committing a war crime by Nobel Peace Prize–winner Doctors Without Borders!

That's crazy—and that's how destroyed America, as a global brand, has become under this terrible, terrible Obama administration!

We have a tall order ahead of us!

That's why bold moves will stun the world—especially after two terms of Bush II's stupidity and two terms of Obama's weakness!

That's why returning Guantánamo to Cuba is a bold move.

I have to say that I was influenced by Patrick Buchanan's book *Death of the West.*

He anticipates the death of America if we continue down this path—and Hillary Hippo Hips Hypocrite, the Pied Piper of Pathos, will continue to lead American down the road to perdition!

She's been a disaster in everything she has ever done!

First Lady: disaster!

U.S. Senator for New York: disaster!

Presidential candidate against that Kenyan Socialist in 2008: disaster!

Secretary of State: disaster!

And, I will point out now, her campaign is a disastrous mess—her numbers are tanking when you compare her poll numbers with the fortune she's squandering!

But we can turn this around. We can turn things around so the nightmare of the Bush II and Obama eras of mediocrity and failure are things of the past.

When I get to Washington, I assure you the economy's going to be just absolutely like a rocket. This is what I'm good at, this is really my wheelhouse.

I will get the world to respect us again!

I will restore America the Brand!

America the Beautiful is one thing, but America the Powerful is another.

Don't dream it. Be it.

America the Powerful is America the Brand!

Make America Great Again!

Vote Trump.

17. Politicians Can No Longer Bamboozle the American Public

Our leaders are stupid!

They're stupid to think that the American public is stupid!

Yes, we've been fooled by politicians—from both parties, but mostly by the Democrats.

I've already addressed the huge, huge, huge problem of Democrats using political correctness as a weapon to attack Latinos.

It's true.

But Democrats, as their modus operandi, deceive the public by *following* and not *leading*.

We elect men and women—and, when we're out of collective minds, intersex persons—to public office to lead.

And what do they end up doing?

They end up following!

They don't *lead!* They *follow!*

They follow opinion polls. They follow television ratings. They follow declarations that pundits make. They follow what's trending on Twitter. They follow, even, *People* magazine!

Then, after all that following, they turn around and try to brainwash the public into thinking that what's trending, leading, high in the polls, and soaring in the ratings is their own!

It's true.

Take, for instance, gay marriage.

Everyone—Republican and Democrat *alike*—was opposed to same-sex marriage.

We just didn't think that it was what we wanted to do in our society.

If you want two men or two women to get married, move to Amsterdam—where prostitution is legal and so are drugs.

Those, quite frankly, are three reasons the Netherlands is never going to be a superpower.

Then, in a decision that was not surprising, but certainly a game changer, the Supreme Court ruled that Americans have the right to marry people of their own gender.

With that—agree or disagree—same-sex marriage became the law of the land.

So now that the Supreme Court ruled, opponents of same-sex marriage have to work within the context of that new *reality*. And if they want to go back, I think it's almost impossible.

But whether you agree or disagree with that decision, now look at how the Democrats—like the duplicitous cheats that they are—are turning things around.

They have introduced a new narrative!

The Democrats are now saying that they were in *favor* of same-sex marriage all along!

May I remind the American people that it was Bill Clinton who, back in 1996, signed the Defense of Marriage Act. The Defense of Marriage Act was a United States federal law that defined marriage, for federal purposes, as the union of one man and one woman, and allowed individual states to refuse to recognize same-sex marriages granted under the laws of other states.

In other words, Bill Clinton signed a law that legalized *discrimination* against gays and lesbians.

There's more: Section 3 of the Defense of Marriage Act barred same-sex married couples from being recognized as spouses under the law for purposes of federal benefits. This, in effect, barred same-sex couples from receiving all federal marriage benefits.

Let's be clear about this: Bill Clinton signed a law that authorized the federal government to discriminate against same-sex couples.

But if you hear Hillary Hippo Hips Hypocrite, she's been fighting for same-sex marriage all her life!

What bullshit!

Yes, that's what it is: bullshit.

And it's a brazen attempt to run away from her prior position: supporting legislation that discriminated against same-sex couples and fought to prevent same-sex marriage.

Of course, Obama, you may have forgotten, also supported the Defense of Marriage Act when it was passed into law.

You wouldn't think that was the case to hear him now.

Wasn't he the first president—in the summer 2015—to light up the White House in the colors of the Gay Pride flag?

Yes!

He was!

The fucking White House looked like a huge billboard for the Life Savers brand of hard candy.

And now, he takes credit for the legalization of same-sex marriage and touts it as an achievement of his administration—just to garner favor with the LGBTQ community—as if he had been pushing for same-sex marriage all along.

But do you remember how he explained his opposition to same-sex marriage?

I have it right here! This is what he said: "What I believe is that marriage is between a man and a woman. . . . What I believe, in my faith, is that a man and a woman, when they get married, are performing something before God, and it's not simply the two persons who are meeting."

That's what Barack Obama, who lit up the White House in the colors of Gay Pride flag, said he believed.

He *opposed* same-sex marriage based on his religious beliefs.

Do you see?

Do you see how the Democrats want to rewrite history?

Hillary Clinton and Barack Obama want you to believe they *led* on this issue.

They didn't *lead*. They *followed*.

They *followed* the decision of the Supreme Court!

Well, my fellow Americans, when Americans go to the voting booth, they are voting for *leaders*—not *followers!*

Hillary Rotten-to-the-Core Clinton is a follower!

She's not a leader!

And the Democrats are equally duplicitous about everything!

Do I have to give you another example?

How about the right of gays and lesbians to serve in the military?

Hillary Clinton addressed the Human Rights Campaign in Washington, D.C., in October 2015 and declared that transgender people have the right to serve in the military.

That's what she said.

The military, where everyone, regardless of their genitalia, wears a uniform is now supposed to accommodate intersex soldiers?

What does that mean?

If everyone is in uniform, what difference does it make?

A woman pulling a Chaz Bono or a man going the way of Caitlyn Jenner—how would anyone know when everyone's wearing camouflage and combat boots?

Now, Hillary Hippo Hips Hypocrite *pretends* to be a cheerleader for the Lesbians, Gays, Bisexuals, Transgenders, and Queers— LGBTQs—enlisted in the military. She's pretending to have changed her tune simply because she's pandering to LGBTQ voters. She says she changed her mind, but she's lying. She just needs their votes.

She changed her mind because it is politically expedient to change her mind.

Why do I say this?

May I remind you?

May I remind you that it was her husband who had Don't Ask, Don't Tell as policy?

Isn't that hypocrisy?

"Don't tell me you're gay!" the military was asked to say.

"Don't tell anyone I'm gay!" members of the LGBTQ community reminded themselves every day.

Isn't that hypocrisy?

Isn't that a national policy of self-deception and self-deceit?

Yes, it is!

In fact, Don't Ask, Don't Tell was the official federal policy on service by members of the LGBTQ community instituted by Bill Clinton on February 28, 1994. This policy of self-deception and self-deceit prohibited military personnel from discriminating against or harassing closeted LGBTQ persons while barring those who were out from enlisting in the military.

In other words, if you're lying—and a closet case—that's fine, but if you're honest and openly gay, then you're thrown out.

To Bill and Hillary Clinton, lies were fine, but the truth was not.

Sounds like their marriage!

And it sounds like the Democratic Party!

You see, that's how Democrats govern: deception, deceit, and hypocrisy.

Let's go back to the 1980s.

Remember the ozone hole over Antarctica?

May I remind you of Dianne Feinstein?

She pretended to be so concerned about the ozone hole, but she, personally, used so much hair spray that she was, probably, the person who single-handedly released more fluorocarbons into the atmosphere than anybody else in the world!

Take a look at a picture of her from that time!

That's not a hairdo: that's a black enamel helmet on her head, that wretched wench!

And this sort of hypocrisy and flip-flopping is the way these politicians bamboozle the American public.

When Clinton was president, he signed into law the most repressive and oppressive laws that harmed the interests of gays and lesbians.

Now, Hillary is getting ready to dance naked on a Gay Pride float down Fifth Avenue in New York City while Lady Gaga eats her pussy!

That's how desperate she is to bamboozle the LGBTQ community.

Be honest!

Hillary Hippo Hips Hypocrite was against same-sex marriage most of her life! She was against members of the LGBTQ community serving opening in the military most of her life!

Are you surprised? Are you surprised, America?

I'm not.

It's what I would expect from a *follower*—and Hillary Hippo Hips Hypocrite is now, has always been, and will forever remain a FOLLOWER!

She's a follower! She follows what's most politically expedient! She has no convictions! She's a follower!

I'm a leader.

And I will tell you what I think and what I believe without having to commission an opinion poll first.

And what do I believe?

I believe that the United States of America is a Judeo-Christian country. That's who we are as a people and as a nation.

Do we welcome others? Of course!

We have no problem with Buddhists, Hindus, Muslims, Wiccans, or atheists.

But, at our core, we are a Judeo-Christian nation—and our national institutions reflect this fundamental truth.

And because we are a Judeo-Christian nation, we have an obligation to protect our society, to safeguard the essence of American culture.

What do I mean?

I mean that we have the right to limit, say, Haitian immigrants who want to practice voodoo. Why? Because sacrificing chickens for religious practices runs counter to the ideals we cherish as advocated by the Society for the Prevention of Cruelty to Animals. We also stand against extremists who are on the fringe of recognized religion, such as the Zion Coptics, who want to smoke nonmedicinal marijuana as part of their religious freedom.

We take these kinds of stands all the time.

Christian Scientists, who denounce modern medicine, are hauled off to court if they try to prevent doctors from treating their sick children. Hasidic Jews are not permitted to keep their daughters illiterate by keeping them out of schools.

Christian Scientists are nuts and are routinely jailed when they violate court orders. Hasidic Jews want to live in a theocracy that is at odds with our way of life.

They may be Christians and Jews, but they are on the fringe—and the law steps in to prevent them from creating communities in this country that harken back to the medieval times of ignorance and superstition.

You know where I'm going. You know what group I'm going to talk about now.

I have no problem with Muslims. I'd have a Muslim in my cabinet. I have hundreds of Muslim employees. But I have moderate and secular Muslims working for me—not radical extremists.

And that's the way business is run.

If you're successful, you're successful because you're tolerant, nonjudgmental, and practical.

Remember the Twin Towers?

Did you know there were so many Muslims who worked or had business in the Twin Towers that, in the South Tower, on the 17th floor, there was a Muslim prayer room?

It's true.

There was a Muslim prayer room, open to the public, on the 17th floor of the South Tower—and there was no controversy at all.

Why?

Because no one cared.

Why?

Because the Muslims at the Twin Towers were, like the majority of Muslims around the world, normal people living in peace and minding their own business.

But that all changed on September 11, 2001.

Quite frankly, I don't see the people who knocked down the

World Trade Center going back to Sweden. Right?

So we *do* have a problem with Muslim extremists in this country the way we have problem with Christian extremists—like Christian Scientists—who want to deny their children lifesaving medical treatments.

I think a segment of Muslims in our country today are certainly a problem, unless you want to be so politically correct where you want me to say, "Oh, absolutely not."

I'm going to say what we all think: Muslim extremists—the ones who want to blow themselves up to kill innocents, the ones beheading people, the ones shouting "Death to America"—are a national security concern for us.

At a campaign rally in New Hampshire, a man stood up and asked a question.

"We have a problem in this country," he said. "It's called Muslims."

Then he said that the president was not Christian. He said this mistakenly, by the way, since I believe Barack Obama when he says he's a Christian.

The man, in fact, said, "You know our current president is one. You know he's not even an American."

And then, Josh Earnest, White House spokesman, attacks me.

"The people who hold these offensive views are part of Mr. Trump's base," he said.

Offensive views?

Is John Earnest saying that it's offensive for someone to say, mistakenly, that Barack Obama is a Muslim?

What if he were a Muslim? Would that be *offensive?* Josh Earnest, the anti-Muslim bigot, just said so!

I think Josh Earnest *proved* himself to be an anti-Muslim bigot!

There's nothing *offensive* about being a Muslim—Hillary Hippo Hips Hypocrite loves a Muslim aide so much she is on record as saying she considers her staffer to be like a daughter to her!

Then, Josh Earnest continues: "It is too bad that he wasn't able to summon the same kind of patriotism that we saw from Senator McCain, who responded much more effectively and directly when one of his supporters at one of his campaign events seven years ago raised the same kind of false claims."

Someone mistakenly believes Barack Obama is a Muslim and this is a "false claim" and "unpatriotic"?

Give *me* a break! Give *America* a break!

Josh Earnest is a pathetic drama queen, isn't that the case? He's just another hysterical drama queen feigning mock outrage!

Of course, no one is better at feigning mock outrage than Hillary Clinton.

Do you know what she said?

She opened her mouth and said, "His latest outrage, the way he handled the question about President Obama, was shocking but not surprising. He" — *meaning me* — "has been trafficking in prejudice and paranoia throughout this campaign."

Really?

All I did was to allow a man to ask a question — and now I'm at fault because the man asking the question was mistaken about whether Barack Obama goes to a church, a synagogue, or a mosque?

Who cares?

Isn't that who we are as a people?

I was taught that freedom of religion meant you really didn't care where other people went to pray or how they prayed.

Am I morally obligated to defend the president every time somebody says something bad or controversial about him? I don't think so!

If I had challenged the man, the media would have accused me of interfering with that man's right of free speech. A no-win situation!

And, quite frankly, if someone made a nasty or controversial statement about me to the president, do you really think he would come to my rescue?

No chance!

This is the first time in my life that I have caused controversy by NOT saying something.

What Josh Earnest—and, by implication, Barack Obama—and Hillary Clinton want to do here is to bamboozle the American public!

They want to use the anti-Muslim sentiment that exists out there as a weapon against me to invent some bigotry that isn't there!

Do you know how I know there was a Muslim prayer room on the 17th floor of the South Tower?

I know that because, on two occasions, I went there.

I had a business meeting in the Twin Towers, and one of my associates was Muslim and he showed it to me. It was like any other place of worship, a boring and mostly empty room.

Big yawn. That's how boring it was. That's why I, a Presbyterian, seldom attend church. Big yawn.

I want to know how many times Hillary Hippo Hips Hypocrite went to the Muslim prayer room in the World Trade Center before the Twin Towers were blown up by Muslim extremists!

I know the answer: NEVER!

That reprehensible charlatan—who, by the way, was nothing but a pathetic carpetbagger when she served as U.S. senator from New York—never, ever went to the Muslim prayer room in the South Tower!

In the same way she now pretends to be a champion for same-sex marriage and members of the LGBTQ community who want to serve openly in the military, she is now fabricating something about me.

Believe me, Joan Didion—in perhaps the only coherent thing that wreck of a wench has ever written—got it right. Joan Didion said, "Everybody knows that what you see in politics is fake or confected. But everyone is Okay with that, because it's all been focus-grouped."

Josh Earnest and Hillary Clinton are focus-grouped phonies!

Is it any wonder that, as I travel this great country—our country that will be great again after I'm elected—I see nothing but outrage and the contempt the American people have for the Democrats!

Can you blame the American people?

I don't!

How can anyone have anything but disgust and contempt for Hillary Clinton, who has fashioned a career from deceit, deception, and bamboozling the American people?

She's so in favor of same-sex marriage that she supported her husband signing the Defense of Marriage Act! Hypocrite! She's so in favor of LGBTQ members in the military serving openly that she supported her husband's "Don't Ask, Don't Tell" policy. Hypocrite!

She's so in favor of Latinos that she was secretary of state for Barack Obama, the man who's deported more Latinos than any other president in American history!

Hypocrite!

It's disgusting, that's how reprehensible she is!

Obama is an enemy of Latinos—as confirmed by his reprehensible, despicable, and hateful actions that have harmed the interests of Latinos!

I'm not a politician.

I have *not* built a career on bamboozling the American people. That's what sets me apart from the others running! That's why I'm killing it in the polls!

In fact, back in the 1970s, another Republican president, Richard Nixon, saw in me the promise of being a great Republican candidate.

Did you know that?

Did you know that Richard Nixon and I were pen pals?

Well, we were.

And do you know what President Nixon wrote to me? He sent me a letter that said, "As you can imagine, Pat Nixon is an expert on politics, and she predicts that whenever you decide to run for office, you will be a winner!"

It's true.

Pat Nixon recognized that I have what it takes to be a great Republican leader.

And isn't that what this election is all about? ELECTING A LEADER, NOT A FOLLOWER!

I will lead and I will speak the truth.

And the truth is that while the Democrats are too busy worrying about this slight or that slight to the hypersensitive Muslims throughout the world, it is Christians who are under assault!

Christians need support in our country—and around the world—because the lives of Christians are at stake!

In Iraq, ISIS is crucifying Christians.

In Egypt, terrorists are bombing churches.

Where is the outrage?

Europe is being asked to take in one million—yes, one million—Syrian refugees, but what about the Christians under attack?

Remember those savages in Libya?

They abducted and beheaded Christians!

Christians are being attacked—and *slaughtered*—around the world. Even Pope Francis has called on Christian nations to defend Christians.

It's true!

When Starbucks changed its holiday cup, it's an affront to Christmas.

Christians are tired at having to apologize for their holidays!

Easter is not about a bunny! It's about the resurrection of Christ. Christmas is not an end-of-year holiday based on Saturnalia, but the celebration of the birth of Christ!

If we remove Christmas from the "Holiday Season," then we are censoring Christians.

Would we do this to other religions?

How would Jews feel if the themes of atonement and repentance were removed from Yom Kippur and it was celebrated as National Juice Fast Day?

If Obama is really a Christian, as he says he is, well, then that means that he's the most powerful Christian in the world.

And don't you think that the most powerful Christian in the

world has the moral obligation—and *religious* duty—to do everything he can to protect Christians who are under attack?

Obama has been horrible!

I will be great!

And I will be great because I am not a politician. I have not made a career out of bamboozling the American people! I have not used political spin as a way of life!

Deception is not my modus operandi!

And America is tired of politicians who spin, deceive, and bamboozle.

That's why we're no longer a great country: We have been spun, deceived, and bamboozled into the ground, where jobs are shipped overseas and our nation grows more indebted with every passing hour.

Unbelievable!

Give *me* a break! Give *America* a break!

Don't let that giant, fat blue robin deceive you: Hillary Clinton was *against* same-sex marriage and *for* Don't Ask, Don't Tell until she had no choice but to *follow* the Supreme Court.

She's a follower! She's a pathetic follower!

I will lead!

I will lead, because Americans want a leader!

I am a LEADER!

Make America Great Again!

Vote Trump.

Make Trump Great Again.

Vote, America!

About the Author

Franco "Pancho" Bahamonde, no relation to the dictator, is a political commentator and satirist. When not being sardonic, he enjoys a gracious life in the García Ginerés, a community established by a relation, the renowned real estate developer Joaquín García Ginerés.

This is his first English-language work designed to interfere in the internal affairs of the United States of America—in violation of the founding charter of the United Nations.

A Note from the Publisher

Proceeds from the sale of this book are being donated to help Hispanic, Latino, and Latin American youth continue their education.